Seasons Change

SUSAN KAY

iUniverse, Inc.
Bloomington

Seasons Change

This is a work of fiction. All of the characters, names, incidents, organizations, and dialogue in this novel are either the products of the author's imagination or are used fictitiously.

iUniverse books may be ordered through booksellers or by contacting:

iUniverse
1663 Liberty Drive
Bloomington, IN 47403
www.iuniverse.com
1-800-Authors (1-800-288-4677)

ISBN: 978-1-4759-8474-3 (sc)
ISBN: 978-1-4759-8476-7 (hc)
ISBN: 978-1-4759-8475-0 (ebk)

Printed in the United States of America

iUniverse rev. date: 04/25/2013

This book is being dedicated to the one of the most incredible women I have ever known and the influence that she has had on and in my life. My mother, Eleanor Scottie Mills, September 5, 1935-May 9, 2009. I love you mom, thanks for everything. I write because of you. Also to my three daughters Whitney, Kalyn and Ailisha whom God has blessed me with although some days have been challenges, God has always seen us through to tomorrow. Keep following your dreams, because the only closed door is the one we never really try to open.

Chapter 1

● ● ● ● ● ● ● ● ● ● ● ● ● ● ● ● ● ● ● ●

It was the hot end of May, and Tiffany was going to things settled once and for all with Jordan. She was tired of his back and forth with the way he felt about her. One minute it was I love you, and the next it was slow down we are moving too fast. Tiffany had to know what was really going on with them. They had been going out since they were fifteen and Jordan was also the only guy that she had ever been with, not that other guys were not looking and offering but, what was not to look at five nine mahogany brown long naturally wavy hair with light brown highlights in which most of the time she wore brushed back behind a headband, golden camel brown skin and eyes so dark you would think they were black onyx jewels, which always seemed to shine when she walked in a room, she looked good coming in and coming out of a room, because the view from behind was just as breath taking. Jordan on the other hand had been with a few girls; let's just say he knew what to do when it came to women.

They were eighteen and in a few weeks graduating from high school. Jordan knew what he wanted to do with his life, he wanted to play in the NBA and he had the athletic ability to get him there. He was the starting center and team captain both his junior and senior years; he stood six three, two hundred twenty pounds of lean well toned and sculpted

1

muscle, milk chocolate skin, with eyes that were dark brown that you could fall asleep in every night just knowing that they meant love and would be looking at you forever. The only thing was that he either had his eyes on his game or on Brooklyn Northgate, Ms. Head Cheerleader, who had the right moves and could get any guy she set her sights on, and right now it seemed as if her sights were on Jordan. Brooklyn was pretty, five five with beautiful long black hair that she wore straight and down usually covering one eye just to add to her mystery and suspense as she looked over the room spotting her next victim, and the way she was built any man would take a second, third and forth look at her. She always seemed to have it in for Tiffany, because Tiffany had only been a cheerleader for one year and she had been asked by the cheerleading coach to come up with routines for the last two games, and she overlooked Brooklyn being the cheerleading captain, which led to bad feeling between the two of them. Well at least bad feelings for Tiffany from Brooklyn, who always let her feeling known around everyone, especially the other cheerleaders.

Jordan just really seemed preoccupied lately, why not all the notes from other girls, the arguments that never seem to get a resolution, the phone numbers in his pocket or left in his locker, all the times that he was not where he said he was going to be, and always just being a million miles away when they were together, it was just starting to get old. To top it off was last night the argument the two of them had was stupid. It was Thursday night before finals and Tiffany had gone over to Jordan's house to study for the Accounting finals and watch a movie. In the middle of the movie his phone rang on the phone stand next to Tiffany, Jordan leaned over to answers it, and then just got up and went into the other room and closed the door to finish his conversation. He returned to the room about fifteen minutes later, "So we have secrets now? You can't talk in front of me? What's her name . . . Brooklyn? You don't think I seen the two of you in the hallway at school

today? I didn't know that you knew CPR, as close as the two of you where, I was only guessing that she was chocking on something and you were helping her get it out of her throat! Better yet just take me home and call Brooklyn back and tell her to come over, she won!" Tiffany shouted as she just stormed out of the house.

Jordan ran after her, "Tiffany just hold on, you were watching the movie and I didn't want to disturb you. There is nothing going on between me and Brooklyn, she's just a friend. We went out before true, but that was the past and that is where I'd like for her to stay. Trust me Baby that road has been traveled on by too many people, and if everybody's had it, why do I want it? Come on girl get back in the house, you need to give me some lovin'. You know the kind that both of us know you came here for. Beside that baby, you know I love you. So quit trippin' and get back in this house so we can do what you came here for. You know that my mom is gone all week, so it can be you and me all week day and night." Jordan said as he took Tiffany by the arm and tried to pull her close to him.

"Jordan let me go. I came over here to study for finals and watch a movie, not to try and make out. I just wanted to watch a movie. You know just be with you. No sex! Is that all there is between us now?" Tiffany said pulling away. "Let me go. I'm just going to walk home. Jordan will you please just let me go? I have too much on my mind to have to go through all of this with you right now. See you tomorrow." She pulled away from Jordan and began walking down the street.

Five blocks down the street, Tiffany said to herself, "I have to know for myself, so that I will know what my next move needs to be." Tiffany walked into the drugstore, which was just about to close.

As she entered the store the manager said, "Miss, we will be closing in about ten minutes so you need to hurry up and make your purchase." She rushed down the isles looking up and down for feminine products. Here it is right down isle

3

four, pregnancy test. Just touching the box, her stomach was turning. Just the thought that she could be pregnant just blew her mind. "What was Jordan going to say? Would he want me to keep it or to have an abortion? Would he be ready to be a father?" She picked up the box and went to the checkout.

"That will be nine dollars and fifty nine cents please." The cashier said in one of those I am ready to get out of here sounding voices.

Seven more blocks she would be home. I am not going to answer the phone if it rings because I know that it will be Jordan and I have nothing else to say to him right now, all I need is a little time to think. "What's he going to think if I am pregnant? Does he really love me? Will he help take care of the baby, or just try to think I'm trying to trap him? What about school, college the whole nine yards? My dad is going to kill me and then he will try and castrate Jordan. God what am I going to do, please help me!" Finally home, she went upstairs to her room, got dressed for bed and, took the pregnancy test out of her purse. "God, please don't let this test turn out to be positive." Tiffany said as she placed the package on the night stand by her bed, then got into bed and turned off the light.

Next thing she knew it was morning, dad yelled up the stairs "Come on sleepy head your going to be late for your finals at school. You need to get up and get dressed."

"I'm up! I'm up!" Tiffany yelled back at him, burying her head back in her pillow.

"Do you want some eggs and bacon? I'm cooking and you know that does not happen very often, so take advantage." Dad said.

Tiffany reached over and grabbed the pregnancy test. She could feel her heart start racing. She opened the box and took the test out of the package. "Here I go," Tiffany said and off to the bathroom she went, so nervous that she could hardly even pee. "God give me strength, please give me strength." Tiffany said out loud.

Just then her dad knocked on the door, "Are you okay in there?"

"Yes Dad, how is my breakfast coming?" Tiffany said in an attempt to get him away from the door and back down the stairs cooking a breakfast that her nerves probably would not even allow her to eat. Dad went back down the stairs to finish cooking.

"Damn it! It's positive." She shouted as the tears started to run down my face. "What is Jordan going to say? He is going to think I am trying to trap him, and that is not what I want to do, I love him. I need to get myself together. I've got finals in an hour, then graduation next weekend. Oh my God, my dad is going to kill me." Tiffany thought to herself. "Come on Tiff you can do this." She said standing and wiping the tears from her face as she looked in the bathroom mirror at herself. She got dressed and headed down stairs. Dad had it all laid out, bacon, eggs, toast and orange juice on the side. "Wow Dad what's going on, this looks great! Okay Dad who is she, and when do I get to meet her?" Tiffany said picking up a piece of bacon.

"Well, Miss, her name is Michelle and you will meet her this evening at dinner. Now come on let's get out of here so you wont be late for those finals, my soon to graduating baby." Ken said opening up the front door.

"Thanks dad for the ride to school and for breakfast, it was good. I can't wait to meet Michelle. It's about time you found someone, you deserve to be happy, and by the way you are acting looks like she does that" Tiffany said as she closed the door to his new black caddy.

He rolled down the passenger side window before he pulled off, "Have a good one, and don't forget about dinner this evening. Love you" and off he went.

As Ken pulled away Tiffany's History teacher Ms. Julie Cotton walked up next to her and said, "Girl one of these days you are going to be calling me mom, your daddy looks so good. Yes, and one day you're going to make me a fine husband. Too bad he does not know it yet." She smiled as she patted Tiffany on the shoulder.

Ken was a keeper, he stood six foot two well built and always stylishly dressed. Since Tiffany's mom Eleanor, had died three years ago, he was always working trying to make sure that we had everything that we needed, even if it meant him working his ass off to do it. Just to make sure that I did not miss the void in my life from not having my mom there to go to. I just hope that Michelle will be the right one for him and not just after his money. I remember Ms. Terry West came in smiling, and took dad for a lot. I just hope that I get a chance to talk to dad before dinner and that he won't kill me, when he finds out I'm pregnant. "Focus Tiffany focus", she said to herself as she made her way to the building. There was Jordan leaning against the building with his boys. I'm sure making their plans for the week and the weekend with his mom gone.

"Hey Tiff?" with a slight tilt of his head that said come on over here.

"Hey yourself." as she just walked past hoping that he could not see the look of oh my God I have something to tell you, written all over her face.

Thank God I made it into the building before he could stop me she thought to herself. Just then the bell rang to go inside. Room 217 Mr. Anderson class, Accounting. As the students came in, he stood in the front of the class with the exam in his hands; waiting for us to come in and be seated. Tiffany got done in record time and moved onto the next exam room, 227 Mrs. Fields, English exam, and then 131 Mrs. Jackson's Biology exam, then she was done. She walked past another room and saw that Jordan was still taking one of his exams, he looked up in her direction and gave her a wink, but had to get back to work on his exam. She was able to make it home just in time to hear the phone ringing. I can't do this not now, not over the phone. It has to be face to face, so that I can see Jordan's face. So she just let the answering machine pick up thinking "Jordan you will understand when we talk, I just can't do it now. Not over the phone." She decided to go upstairs to take a long hot bath, she figured dad would be home soon, and they would get a chance to talk before dinner. She jumped in the tub and she heard the phone ringing again so she turned up the music to her cassette player, and laid back in the tub to try and relax. When she was ready to get out of the tub, she turned the music off, and she heard someone yelling outside. It was Jordan and he looked mad.

"You want to play games, then games is what we will play! .... and I'll win this shit!" He yelled as he got in his car and slammed the door with tires screeching drove away.

"Oh God what have I done? He is so mad at me now. He will never forgive me for not answering the door." Tiffany said crying. I need to call him and say something, anything to him and make him understand. Tiffany waited a few minutes and called Jordan's house. His brother, Michael answered the phone and said that he was not home, but he would tell him that I called. Tiffany thought to herself, Jordan is not coming home tonight. He is going to find some house party or he will have one himself, since his mom was gone for the weekend and all next week, but as long as they are in church on Sunday morning in Grandma Ellen's eyes her grandsons were perfect little angels, and she would not have to report anything wrong back to their mom when she came back. Just then dad pulled up in the driveway. Let me paint this fake smile on my face and enjoy dad's happiness.

"Hey Tiffany, are you ready?" Dad yelled from down stairs.

"Yeah dad I'll be right there." Tiffany replied. Tiffany walked outside and went to the front door, not noticing that dad's date Michelle was already in the car. She opened the front door, "Oh .... I'm sorry I did not notice anyone in the car." Tiffany said closing the front door and getting in the back seat of the car.

Dinner was fine, but Tiffany could since that dad knew something was wrong. I hope that he won't think that it's Michelle, or it was the fact that in the morning he and Michelle were going to drive to Memphis to visit with my grandma without me.

Dad took Tiffany home after dinner and told Tiffany that he would be back in a little while, then said that they would talk when he got back.

When he got back, Tiffany had already fallen asleep, so he didn't bother waking her.

The next morning she was up early and said to herself that she was going to get this over with. She asked her dad to borrow his car for a couple of hours, because she knew he got in late and he was going to do nothing but sleep until at least ten if not later, then he would hit the road with Michelle, to see Grandma in Memphis. That will give me time enough to talk to Jordan she thought to herself. And dialed Jordan's number, the phone rang, but no one answered. She thought she would just run to the store, and by the time she got done he would be back at home and they could talk. In the store, the morning sickness or nerves started to take over; everything just looked like an upset stomach ready to happen. She left out and thought enough is enough; I'll just go by and see for myself if he is home. Just like she thought in the driveway there sat his Volkswagen Rabbit bright white. "That bastard, he knew it was me and he's just avoiding my calls!" she yelled inside, her father's car. Her stomach began to turn in knots as she parked. "I'm just going to come right out and tell him and see what he says." She knocked on the front door, but no answer, then she heard laughter coming from the back yard, she walked around to the back of the house, in the yard stood Jordan and Brooklyn, laughing and holding each other like they were just to in love to let go of each other. "How could you? How could you do this to me, to us and to our baby? I am pregnant you stupid son of a bitch!" Tiffany screamed as the tears just ran down her face, and with that she turned around and ran to her dads car and drove off. She could see Jordan running behind the car yelling for her to come back.

"Baby, pregnant, what the hell did you just say? Tiffany bring your ass back here we need to talk!" As he ran screaming off behind her leaving Brooklyn standing there looking pissed off and confused. He stops chasing after Tiffany and turned around and saw Brooklyn standing there along with one of her girlfriends. "Hey Brooklyn I'm sorry but you and your girls are going to have go. I'm sorry about last night, it was a mistake. I have to go and talk to Tiffany and find out about my . . . . our baby. The girl says she's pregnant . . . . Brooklyn I'm sorry I have to go."

* * *

She could hardly stop crying long enough to make it home, but as soon as she pulled into the driveway her dad was standing outside, like he knew what happened and was just standing there. "What's wrong?" He said with his overly protective father voice, as he walked over to her and put his arms around her.

They went inside the house where Tiffany explained everything to him and crying nonstop with every word.

"Pregnant! Haven't I talked to you until I'm blue in the face about birth control? Now what? What are you going to do? What about graduation next weekend and college? No one wants to have a child with a child living in the dorms with them. Tiffany you should have been more careful. Boys his age only want one thing, and I guess he got that from you, and now he has moved on to his next trophy." Ken said with his angry voice.

"I don't know dad, I can't have an abortion. I don't know, everything is happening so fast. I just found out myself yesterday. I don't know. Jordan is already seeing someone else and does not want me. I caught him this morning with

Brooklyn Northgate in his backyard. I am so stupid, what am I going to do?" Tiffany said looking to dad for answers.

"Hell I don't know. I think that we need to take a step back and look at the whole picture. You know I told you that Michelle and I were going to Memphis for the week; maybe you should come with us. It'll be fun and it will give you a better chance to get to know Michelle and take your mind off of everything going on. Beside that your Grandma maybe able to shed some light on your situation and give you some good advice." He said fatherly.

"That will be good I have not seen Grandma in a while. I just need to pack a few things." Tiffany said quietly.

"Hurry up and pack and then we'll go and get Michelle, she should be just about ready to go by now, all I need to do is call and check." Ken said standing up and heading to the phone to call Michelle.

About an hour later they were all packed and leaving out the door to get Michelle, and then on the road. As they were walking out the door the phone began to ring, it took everything in Tiffany not to pick it up, because she knew that it would be Jordan on the other end and then she would come up with some excuse as of why she needed to stay. "Come on young lady. You need this, you need to get away and think about what you want to do for yourself and not have someone else tell you what you are supposed to do. Come on now pick up your purse and let's go." Ken yelled from outside. "Let's get this show on the road."

Chapter 2

• • • • • • • • • • • • • • • • • • • •

Grandma's house seemed so peaceful and quiet; you know the type of house that when you walk in you feel like you are being hugged before anyone even says anything to you. "Surprise Grandma! We were just in the neighborhood and thought we would stop by." Tiffany said just trying to break the ice and the looks that she was getting from Grandma.

"Well, well what brings you all the way down here, something must be wrong for you to come all the way down here and not even a phone call to let me know you're coming?" She said questioning.

"Well Mom I would like you to meet someone. This is Michelle, Michelle Spencer and she is someone very special to me. That is why I want you to meet her. Mom and there is one more thing and I am just going to put it right out there. Tiffany is pregnant and she does not know what to do and wants your advice." Dad said pushing Tiffany closer to Grandma.

"You're what? What about school? What about college? Who's the daddy? What does he want? Does he even . . . .? This is crazy! You are too young to be getting yourself all pregnant and having babies? Girl you have your future all laid out in front of you, and then you go do a thing like this. Have you lost your mind? Don't you go to church, Sunday school believe in God something, or are you just wanting to lay up with some boy? It is just one ain't it?" Grandma said so hatefully and hurtful. "What? The cat got your tongue now?" She said looking over the top of her glasses.

"Dad this was a mistake I should have never come down here! Grandma how can you be so cold, so mean?" Tiffany said, as tears began to fall down her face.

"Come here! Come here gal! Grandma is not trying to hurt you I just wanted so much more for you than I had for myself. I wanted you to find yourself and be independent all on your own without anyone's child to pick up after and care for. You know you have a long road ahead of you now? Don't you? Anyway what about graduation? Isn't that next weekend? What are you going to do? You do have enough of those credit things to graduate, don't you? I love you and always will, you just have to be smarter. Think before you act. Lord I just wish your mother was still alive. This would have never happened." Grandma said.

"Now wait a minute Mom, what are you saying that I am not capable of raising my own daughter? Maybe Tiffany was right, maybe we should not have come down here and have to listen to all of this." Ken responded in a huff.

"Get your underwear out of your ass! I am just saying that she needs her mother, all children do. You are a great provider and protector, but nothing comes closer than a mothers touch. Why do you think you drove all those miles to me once you heard about this?" Grandma said with that look of love in her eyes.

Tiffany walked up the stairs of Grandma's porch and sat down on the steps next to Grandma and laid his head on her knee and just started to cry. "There there Baby that right just let it all out, in the morning we will talk and get everything all work out." Grandma said as she patted Tiffany on the head.

They sat outside until sundown, and then Grandma called them into to get something to eat. After a long silent meal,

Tiffany excused herself and went upstairs to take a shower. All she could think about was Jordan and how he could be so cruel to her at a time when she needed him the most. She reached down and turned off the water and headed to Grandma's room. Tiffany opened the door to Grandma's room to find her already in bed. Tiffany put her night gown on and nestled in the bed right next to Grandma, a place that she knew that she would always feel safe and warm. Just before closing her eyes, and falling asleep, she whispered, "I love you Jordan." and fell right to sleep.

The next day Grandma got up early, early as always and began to cook breakfast, the smell of coffee and bacon filled the house. Oh my God Tiffany thought there was nothing like Grandma's cooking. Nothing better in the world to wake up to then this first thing in the morning.

"Tiffany! Tiffany!" Grandma called out.

As Tiffany came down stairs to her smiling Grandma and found a plate over flowing with eggs, bacon and grits. "Good morning Grandma." Tiffany said as she sat down at the table. "Where are dad and Michelle?" Tiffany asked her Grandma.

Grandma pouring a cup of coffee as she sat at the table next to Tiffany, looked up at her and said, "Tiffany your father wanted you to stay down here for a little while and just talk with me. He and Michelle will be back in a few days. He also thought that it would be a good idea for the school just to mail you your diploma, and not have to deal with all that crazy mess going on back there. He thought that you could use a little bit of alone time. You know time to just set back and think, and figure out what you are going to do with the rest of your life. You know you have to a lot to think about and not that long to figure out what it is that you are going to do. Honey, you know, there is going to be a college and job fair on Monday at the University. Maybe they can show you in what direction you might want to go and what you can do for the two of you, if that is the way you are going to go."

13

"Okay, okay, I know that nothing is going to be a free hand out." Tiffany said with that look of disgust on her face. "Monday I will get up bright and early and head down the road to my future and I know that I will find that open door out there just waiting for me. By the way Grandma can I use your car on Monday? I know where the University is so I won't get lost. I will even put gas in your car too. I just don't know the bus routes here and I would get lost, or not be back until midnight." Tiffany said with that look of please, please Grandma please on her face.

"Of course you can Honey. I will make sure that it has gas in it for you." Grandma said happy that Tiffany had agreed to go.

That Monday morning Tiffany was down the steps and heading to the car. "Hey Grandma I will be back in a little bit", Tiffany said closing the door to the car. Off she went.

Wow she thought as she arrived at the campus this place is beautiful look at all these people. Where will I start? As she parked the car and got out and headed to the first hall. Business after business all handing out applications to be filled out, and all trying to say that their company was better than the next, and that they offered this and that. Tiffany picked up about twelve applications, now onto the next hall. Now this is more like it college after college all telling me that they offered the best classes when it came to accounting and what I needed to have to get into their school, Tiffany picked up about five applications, onto the next hall. Wow military Tiffany thought, I know that I can pass up this hall Army, Navy, Air Force, Marine; I will pass on all of those. Thanks but no thanks. Tiffany saw a hot dog stand and thought to herself I am starving, so she grabbed a hot dog with all the junk on it, and she sat down and began looking over the applications and feeding her face.

"Excuse me miss, is anyone sitting here?" a deep voice came from behind.

Tiffany turned around, and looked up at the tall dark chocolate, clean shaven, fresh hair cut with a well trimmed mustache and so handsome in a uniform that made him look like a walking talking spokes person for the military, stood there, and could anyone join if they could look like that coming out. Where are the paper, let me sign up now, or at least pick one of him out to go. She had to catch herself

"Ahhh . . . . No please sit down take a load off. So what are you Army, Air Force, Navy or Marine?" Tiffany said with a curious smile.

"I am in the Navy." he said, "Just out trying to recruit people today, well actually all week, and you? Are you a student or trying to get people to work at your business?" This tall dark stranger said.

"First of all what is your name? My name is Tiffany and I am out here just trying to find myself and where I want to be." Tiffany said with questioning confidence.

"Well my name is David Morgan, would you like to know more about the Navy? I can get you some brochures and give you a little information about the Navy." David said.

"To be honest with you, I don't know anything about the Navy and I never have been really interested in knowing anything about it. What can they offer me? Tell me Mr. Recruiter; tell me everything and anything you can to make me want to sign up." Tiffany said.

"Well when you get done with your lunch we can go back to my table and I can do my best to sell you on the Navy" Giving Tiffany a look that said I will try and sell you on me and we can just talk about the Navy a little to.

"Okay." Tiffany said

David smiled as if he could stop recruiting and that he had won the one recruit he had been aiming for, and could pat himself on the back and go home. "So are you from Memphis? This is a very busy place, seems like you could just get lost in the crowd and never be able to come up for air." David said trying to make conversation.

"No, I am down here visiting with my Grandmother, I really don't know when I will be going back home or if I want to go back home. You know the life of a teenager not ever knowing what we want but just knowing we need to find it whatever it takes. Then hoping you land on your feet for whatever it brings. I don't know if I want to go to school or if I want to go to work or a little bit of both. I guess Memphis is going to be my home for awhile. As my dad always tells me listen to your Grandma she is the best teacher ever and the older I get the smarter she gets. If I just take the time out and just listen." Tiffany said with a look at David like please just stop me tell me to shut up. "So how long have you been in the Navy and what is your ranking?" Tiffany asked hoping that the focus would be off her for just a few minutes.

"Well I am an AT—Aviation Electronics Technician, but right now I am in charge of recruiting, and yes by the way, I can fly a plain. I have one week to win over a bunch of new recruits, then I am back to Norfolk, Virginia where I am stationed" He said with cocky arrogance.

"Oh really . . . . so when are you going to take me up for a ride?" She answered flirting back. Her stomach started turning as if her unborn child was trying to tell her, mommy slow down daddy won't like this at all. You have to give my real daddy a chance to step up to the plate and be my father." You know I really do need to get out of here, sorry I can't stop by your table and have you tell me all of the wonderful things about the Navy and yourself, but I have to go." She said as she gathered all of her papers together.

"Hey Tiffany can I at least have your phone number so that I can call you and maybe even take you out to dinner or something, or at least a short conversation? Like I said I'm in town for a week, and good company is always a plus for dinner." he said.

"Okay here it is." as she wrote it on a small piece of paper and handed it to him. "Please remember that this is my Grandmother's phone number, so no calling after ten at night.

Hope to hear from you soon Mr. David military man" She said with a kind of shy smile.

"I am sure you will hear from me soon, real soon." Smiling as he placed the number in his uniform pocket.

The only thing that she could think about getting back into her Grandmother's car was Jordan is going to kill me for giving another man the time of day, which then brought tears to her eyes. How could I be so stupid? I need to give Jordan a real chance at being this baby's father. Everyone needs one, look at me, I have the best father anyone could have ever asked for as she pulled out of the parking lot and down the road she drove back to Grandmas. When she finally made it back home, and parked the car she went up to the porch to find Grandma on her porch swing just napping in the Memphis heat. "Hey Grandma, what's going on?" Tiffany said not really wanting an answer.

"Well did you find something to give you the answers that you need? Have you seen a doctor? How far along are you anyway, you don't look very big. In fact, you're not showing at all, are you sure that test was right? What does this young man Jordan even think about becoming a daddy anyway? Girl just what are you going to do? I know that I keep on bugging you, but this baby is real and something that is going to be in your life always." Grandma questioned Tiffany as she placed her velvety soft hand on hers, on what she planned on doing with her life now that she had someone else in it to think about.

"Grandma I got applications for work and for school. My grades where great in high school and my ACT score was 28, I know that when I pick a school to go to, they will want me; my only thing now is that I have to find a school that will take a baby as well as me. I know that a lot of people frown on a girl and baby going to school together, but I want my education and want to be able to give something to my baby whether Jordan is there or not. I am going to be able to provide for my child, so I know that I have to start today."

Tiffany stated with confidence and conviction. Tiffany went into the house leaving Grandma to her porch swing. She looked around at the inside of her house, and the pictures of all the family on the wall and thought to herself, this is what I call living, my Grandma and Grandpa were married fifty-seven years had four children together, and made it work. Even now that my Grandpa is dead my Grandma does not have to worry about anything from anybody, it's like he is still here and looking out for her. She and Grandpa had built that foundation so that if one had to be without the other one, then the other one would still make it. She smiled and continued on up the stairs. "You know little one, mommy has some growing up to do so that we can make it, with or without your father we can make it."

Tiffany said rubbing her still very flat stomach. As she entered in the bedroom, she threw down the papers on the bed and grabbed a pen and began to write. I am just going to have all of these ready for the mailman by tomorrow for him to pickup and hope and pray that someone says yes quickly so that I can start, or so that I can get ready to start. I might even take summer classes down here at the community college. I just need to keep my mind going on school.

Chapter 3

● ● ● ● ● ● ● ● ● ● ● ● ● ● ● ● ● ● ●

The next morning the phone started ringing about nine. "Who could be calling this house so early in the morning on Tuesday "Hello." grandma said looking at the phone "Hold on just a moment I will get her. Tiffany it is someone named David calling wanting to talk to you." Grandma said handing her the phone.

"Hello David. How are you doing? No I don't have any plans this morning. Well I guess I can be ready in about an hour. Sounds like fun; I will see you then."

Tiffany said hanging up the phone. "Grandma, can I use your car if you are not doing anything this morning?" Tiffany asked with the look of please, please Grandma please in her eyes.

"Who is David? Where did you find him? I let you go off by yourself for a few hours and you come back with applications and another man? Child you need to slow down, life is to short don't use it all up chasing men. They only want one thing and you have given enough of yourself up already. Build your foundation for yourself and your child; those are the two people that should mean the most to you. You can use my car, just slow down." She said as she handed her the keys.

"Grandma he is a Navy recruiter, he is only going to be in town for the week and since he knows that I am not from here he is going to take me on a tour of the city and to lunch. See Grandma just a good guy who wants to show me around not lay me down and have his way with me." She said rather defensive. "I love you Grandma and I know. Trust me I know." kissing her Grandma on the cheek. Tiffany headed upstairs to get ready for her day of fun. She picked out a pair of tan walking shorts, a tan tank top, and a very sheer short sleeve button down shirt, to top it off with a nice pair of comfortable walking shoes. No makeup, just lip gloss and pulling her hair back in a ponytail she was ready. As always she had her own money in her purse. Dad said always be prepared to take care of yourself so you don't owe anyone at the end of your days journey. Down the stairs she went. The phone started ringing again. This time she picked it up. "Hello. This is she. Well I guess that will be okay. My address is 4414 Parkview Lane. Oh . . . . okay from where you are it should take you about twenty minutes to get here. Guess I will see you when you get here." She smiled and hung up the phone.

"Grandma I wont need your car after all, David is coming here to pick me up, so you can meet him."

"You watch yourself child. You are giving out my address, planning on spending the day with this young man. All candy is not good candy remember that." Grandma said turning up her nose as she headed into he other room. "All candy is not good" She exclaimed turning the corner.

Oh Grandma, Tiffany thought as she rolled her eyes and sat down on the couch. I can't wait o see him again. David you may just be what I need to get through this trip. Someone that can make me laugh and smile if only for a little while. She thought to herself as her thought started drifting toward Jordan. I hope Brooklyn Northgate is worth my heart being broken and us not being together.

Just then the door bell rang. "Grandma I got it!' Tiffany said heading toward the door.

"Hi David, I see you found the house and by the time, you have a very heavy foot. Did you speed all the way?"

Tiffany laughed looking at her watch and inviting him in. As he stepped in she looked him up and down as he past by. No one should look that good in a pair of shorts and a polo shirt, and smell so manly, the service has done his body real good.

"Hello and how are you doing today? You smell sweet and looking good, if I must say so myself." As David looked at her with a smile that could melt ice and eyes that Tiffany swore could see through her clothes.

Grandma came around the corner. "David I would like you to meet my Grandma, Mattie Miller." Tiffany said nudging Grandma closer.

"How are you young man, my Grandbaby says your name is David? So do you have any people from around here? Or are you one of them old service men that come and go with the tide?" she looked at Tiffany and seen she was looking nervous. "Oh . . . . I am sorry I am forgetting my manors. Would you like to sit down for a bit or do you have big plans for the day with my granddaughter?" Grandma said with a look of curiosity on her face.

"Well Mrs. Miller I am not from around here nor do I have any family here. It is just me alone by myself for the week, and yes I do have the whole day planned out for Tiffany. If I have your permission can I steal her away for the day?" David said with a charming grin on his face, holding his hand out to shake grandma's hand.

"Okay you young people get out of here be safe and be careful." Grandma said as she opened the door for them to leave.

David stepped out ahead and opened the door to his black Olds 88 to let Tiffany in. When she was in her seat, he shut the door behind her, as she turned around and looked up at him with a smile on her face. She quickly clicked the button to unlock the driver's door for him. He kind of chuckled to himself as he got in. "What. What is so funny? Tiffany asked.

"It is something that my mom always told me. Once you open the door and let a lady in the car and she unlocks the door for you, then she is a person that really cares and is worth paying attention to. She just doesn't leave you outside to unlock the door for yourself. And well I see you unlocked the door. You have my undivided attention." David said with that sexy smile.

"Well you have my as well." Tiffany said as she could feel her heart beating faster and faster. "Yes you have mine as well."

That morning and afternoon were spent at museums and art galleries, it was all so breath taking and beautiful she could not believe it. Now for lunch in the park what could be nicer? He had packed it himself as he carried the picnic basket to the perfect spot under a sweet smelling magnolia tree that was just calling out their names. They laughed and talked for hours. The time went by so fast the sun had started to set. "So what are your plans for tomorrow?" David asked.

"I really don't have any plans, unless you have something in mind?" Tiffany said hoping that he would say that he wanted to spend it with her.

"Well I only work until three tomorrow. Would that be too late for us to get together? I really want to see you again. I hope that I am not being too forward or moving too fast? There is just something about you that I can't get out of my mind." David said looking into her eyes. Tiffany began to stand up as David quickly moved to help her up and onto her feet. "So does that mean yes?" David asked questioning.

Tiffany knowing what she should say. "David I really need to spend sometime with my Grandma because I don't get the chance to see her very often. Besides that I really need to get all those papers filled out I picked up at the college fair yesterday and send them off, so my time here is going to be pretty busy. I am sorry, but I do have your number and I will be calling as soon as I get a free minute." Tiffany said looking down at the ground. "Today was really fun and you are a wonderful guy."

"Stop! Stop! I know the "You are a wonderful guy speech." Let's just leave it at we had a good time. You are an amazing woman, I just wish I could say or do something for another chance for a second date with you, but like you said, you have my number, and I will just have to leave it at that." David said taking her hand, and leading down the walk way through the park.

They got to the car and as David opened the door for her, she took him by the hand, "David, wait a minute it's not you it's me. I would like to see you again, I really would, but I have so much going on in my life right now. I don't want to lead you on. I think that that would be wrong, and I'm not that kind of girl, and I don't want you to think that I am." Tiffany said still not making any eye contact.

"I don't understand why you even allowed me to take you out in the first place, that's what I, call leading someone on." David said in disgust.

"Okay then let me tell you the truth. I am pregnant and I just found out myself a few days ago! The guy that I was going out with, I went to tell him and I found him in the arms of another girl in his backyard, and so I just yelled at him and ran away, and so now here I am, in Memphis. Here you are with me, so do you understand where I am coming from? It is not you, not you at all. I mean have you looked at yourself? Damn, what woman wouldn't want to be wined, dined and romanced by you? You have so much to offer a woman. I can't stand in your way. I am sorry." Tiffany said as tears began to roll down her face.

"Hey now take it easy, I didn't mean to make you cry. Sounds like you're in a tough spot." David said as he wiped the tears from her face. "Are you sure you want to go home or would you like to hang out a little longer? Damn girl there are so many questions I want to ask you, but I can see you are already upset and that is the last thing that I want to do is make you even more upset. I just want you to know that I am here if you want to talk. I know that I am only here for a few more days, but I am here.", as he leans over and kisses her on the forehead.

"Thank you David. I . . . . I better get back to grandmas; she will not get any sleep until I make it home safely." Tiffany said looking at the ground.

"To Grandmother's house we go." David sang as he closed the door after Tiffany got in.

The ride home was long and quiet, and then Tiffany broke the silence, "I am sorry. I know you must be thinking that I lead you on, but it really was not like that. Not like that at all. You just seemed so nice and so charming, you make it hard to say "No!" even when I knew I have other things going on in my life that just won't let me be free to enjoy everything that you have to offer. I also want to say, "Thank you, for the wonderful day you planned for me, for us." Tiffany went on to explain the whole story to David about her and Jordan, by the time he pulled up in front of Grandma's, he knew the whole story.

"Hey Tiffany, you have a lot to think about and work through, you need to call him or write him, at least give him a chance to explain, talk and give him a chance to understand because this is about more than just you. The two of you have made something together don't let one mistake tear it apart. Believe it or not that was real hard for me to say that to you, because you are incredible, even with the knowledge of your pregnancy. I still want to spend more time with you and get to know you. Hell girl just to be with you and hang out!" David said holding her face in his hands, and again kissing her forehead. "You are amazing." He got out of the car went around to Tiffany's side to let her out.

Grandma came outside just in time to let David know in her grandmotherly way that it was late and Tiffany needed to get in, as she stepped down the steps of the front porch and said, "Good night young man and thank you for having my baby girl back at a descent hour."

"Yes Ma'am. Thank you for allowing me the honor of taking her away if only for a few hours." David responded as he winked at Tiffany standing on the porch just watching him. Then got back into his car and pulled away. "So how was your day, Miss Tiffany?" Grandma asked looking over the top of her glasses. "Oh Grandma he is . . . . ohhh . . . . Words can't describe the kind of man he is. I also told him that I was pregnant and you know what Grandma? He told me that I needed to talk to Jordan and get an understanding with him. Then he kissed me on the forehead. Wow something so sweet and innocent." Tiffany said with a look of amazement and a sigh of relief in her voice. Grandma I think I am going to go upstairs and write Jordan and let him know what's going on and how I feel. Then I am going to turn in for the night. "Good night Grandma, I love you." Tiffany said as she went into the house and headed up the stairs to begin writing. Dear Jordan . . . After an hour of writing she was done. Everything she wanted to say and everything she wanted to do with or without Jordan. She addressed the envelope put a stamp on it and walked down stairs to the mailbox where she placed the letter to be picked up in the morning. She went back into the house up the stairs and climbed into her bed. "Goodnight David, I hope you are right about this one." Tiffany whispered as she leaned over to turn off the light on the nightstand.

Chapter 4

● ● ● ● ● ● ● ● ● ● ● ● ● ● ● ● ● ●

Tiffany sitting on the front porch, days had gone by since she had mailed the letter to Jordan and no phone call, no letter, no nothing, but lonely hurt feeling just wanting to hear something anything. She heard the front door open Grandma was dressed and heading out the door. "Hey Grandma where are you off to this morning?" Tiffany said as if Grandma had to answer to her.

"I am heading into town for a while; I will probably be back sometime this afternoon, if you really need to know my schedule." Grandma answered just as sarcastic.

"Well you have fun now and stay out of trouble." Tiffany said with a smile.

About an hour later the mail truck pulled up. "How are you doing this morning ma'am?" The postman said handing her the mail.

"I'm doing just fine this morning, thank you sir." Tiffany said responding to his southern hospitality. As she started going through the mail her stomach turned in knots when she saw the letter that she had mailed out to Jordan marked return to sender unopened. How could he, she thought he did not even bother to open and read it. "How could I have been so stupid? How could I have thought that he cared? David, why did I ever listen to you and give Jordan the chance to hurt me again?" Tiffany screamed as she ran in the house. She opened up her purse and pulled out the piece of paper that she had written David's number on. "Please be home. Please be home David, I need to talk to someone. Pick up the phone." She cried out as the phone continued to ring.

"Hello." a voice came through on the other line.

"Hello. May I speak to David?" Tiffany said with a quivering voice.

"This is he" David responded

"Oh David . . . . David this is Tiffany. I am sorry I should not be calling you with my problems, but I couldn't think of anyone else." she said with a cry in her voice.

"What's wrong are you alright?" David said

"I knew I should have never done what you said and write to Jordan." She yelled.

"Why, what happened?"

"It's Jordan, he did not even open the letter, and he just put return to sender on the envelope and mailed it back. How could he be so cruel?" She said crying out of control.

"Hey I have about four hours before I have to start working again. Do you want me to come by to talk?" David asked.

"If it's not going to be any trouble." Tiffany said holding back more tears.

"Give me about twenty minutes and I will be right there. Keep your head up Tiffany, I will be right there." David said hanging up the phone.

About twenty minutes later, Tiffany saw David's car coming down the street, her heart started to race and her mind started to feel comfort as if she knew right away he would make her feel better just by being there. He pulls into the driveway and got out of the car. "What no uniform today? How can you recruit if they can't see how good they are going to look once they sign their name on the dotted line? All joking aside, thanks for coming, you don't know how much this means to me." Tiffany said looking down at the ground.

"A woman crying is never a good or happy sound. Trust me, I heard my mother cry too many times and it was never anything good." He said lifting her head up with his hands. "Now let's find a way to make those sad and hurt feelings go away. Now do want to talk or just want a hug because I'm good at that too."

"Can I have all of the above, starting with a hug?" Tiffany said

"A hug it is." as David wrapped his big strong arms around her delicate body with the smell of morning in her hair and blowing in the wind and dancing on his face.

Arms had never felt so good, strong and comforting. She could have stayed in them forever if only she could or if only he would. "Tiffany there's just something about you that I can't get out of my mind. I was hoping that you would call, but I was going to leave that up to you to make that move. When I answered the phone and heard your voice on the other end, my heart went into my throat. All you had to do was just open the door and as you can see I am here, let me in. So he did not even open the envelope? There must be something more, something that you are not telling me. A man just does not walk away from all of this, and not even turn around for a second chance or even a second look. Tiffany tell me something. There just has to be something." David said looking her in the eyes.

Tiffany went over everything again detail by detail trying to work everything out in her mind about what she could have said, or done. David so understanding just holding her in his arms while she went into detail and cried saying how stupid she must have sounded to him and how dumb she was for believing. David just held onto her as if he would loose her if he loosened his arms from around her, gently kissing her face every time she looked up to him for understanding and comfort. Then without one word spoken he kissed her very gently on the lips. He suddenly pulled back." I'm sorry . . . . I'm sorry Tiffany, you came to me for comfort and now it seems as if I am trying to take advantage of you. I know that we have only known one another for a short time, but I want to fix your world and make you smile. You deserve happiness, you and your little one. You remind me a lot of my mother, she had me when she was sixteen, when my father found out she was pregnant and walked out on her or should I say walked out on us. All he wanted to do was spread his seed and that he did. I have eight brothers and sisters and I was just the beginning. Mom had me and went back to school and went to college, her mind was made up that her baby was never going to have to ask anyone for a handout or to be in anyone's government line waiting for a food stamp or a handout. Yep it is just me and my little brat sister, Karen who thinks she runs the world. Mom has always told her, don't give it away for anything but true love and have patience, not just want easy pleasure. Pleasure has its own price. You know what I mean? I think my dad is still spreading his seed and women are falling for those same old tired lines of his about how much he loves them and only them. Okay, okay enough about me. Are you going to be okay until I get off work tonight and take you out to dinner or go for a drive off into the sunset?" David said with that oh so charming smile on his face.

"David, thank you for coming over. I know that you have to get back to work. You just don't know how you make me feel, and hearing a little bit about your mother, I would love to meet her someday. She sounds like an amazing woman. So dad is a rolling stone? Well some men and women plant better seeds then they can be themselves, and in looking at you, you are one of those seeds. I will be ready when you get off . . . . What time do you get off work?" Tiffany said with a flirty smile.

"I will be done with my recruiting today about six thirty. I don't mind because I feel that you would be worth any wait that I might have." David said as he leaned in and gave her a kiss on the lips.

29

"Until then my sweet, until then." Tiffany muttered to herself as David pulled away in his car.

Tiffany ran into the house. "What to wear? What to wear?" pulling her closet door open. "That's it. This is perfect a sun dress that did not forget about the sun." Tiffany said with a look on her face that said "Yes!" The sun dress was white with large red, yellow and orange flowers dancing everywhere on it, to top it off some beautiful white sandals, high but not too high. "Am I crazy, I just found out that I am pregnant just a few days ago and now I going out on a date with another man." she said scowling at the idea of that. "What is wrong with me? Even better question is, Jordan how could you be such an asshole? Did I really not mean anything to you? How could you be so cruel? You are such a jerk, I am going to move on, because I have two people to think about now!" Tiffany screamed at the top of her lungs. Tiffany went back down stairs to watch a little television before Grandma got back. Before she knew it, she had fallen asleep with the television watching her.

Tiffany awakened to find Grandma back at home looking for her hat as she was preparing to go out on a dinner date. "Wow! Grandma you look good. Where are you on your way to, hot date? Do I know who it is?" Tiffany said questioning grandma with a smile.

"Yes I am going on a dinner date and no you don't know who it is. I should be back about nine or ten tonight. Well no . . . . Let's just say I will be back later on this evening, anymore questions? No . . . . That's what I thought." Grandma said as if to be done with all of the questions and answers she was going to stand for at the moment. "So what are your plans for the night dear?"

"Well David is getting off about six thirty and we are going out to dinner. Grandma stop before you say anything, It is just dinner nothing else. Beside that, I got my answer from Jordan today. I got the letter I wrote him back, return to sender, that's right unopened just return to sender written on the envelope. If that is not an answer, I don't know what is." Tiffany said kind of uppity.

"I'm sorry are you okay baby? I know David seems really nice, just be careful. Slow down and really smell the flowers of life. That's all I am saying." Grandma said looking at Tiffany. "Just slow down baby, life is too short."

"I know Grandma, I am taking my time, now I am going to head up stairs and take a nice long bath and just relax before I get ready. I love you Grandma and I am going to take my time." Tiffany said heading up the stairs to run her bath water.

She laid her sundress on her bed and stepped into the tub. She sat in there for an hour just relaxing and thinking. She knew that it was getting late, so she got out of the tub and got dressed, slipped on her sandals and went down stairs.

David should be here in about twenty minutes. She turned on the television just in time to see the news and here what the weather was going to be. Just beautiful she thought perfect sundress weather. She heard the doorbell ring, her heart started racing, she opened the door and there he stood.

"Hi David." Tiffany said with a smile as bright as the sunrise on her face.

"Hello Tiffany. Looks like you are ready for your evening to begin, or should I say our evening to begin", David said as he took her by the hand and spun her around to enjoy the full view of her body and her dress. "You look amazing! Yes absolutely amazing, and you are all mine for the evening. I will be here to make you laugh and make you smile. I also have one more thing that I hope will surprise you, but I'm saving the best for last."

"Why is that always the way it is, saving the best for last? Tell me or show me now, I don't want to wait for last. Patience you will find I am not good at, not at all." Tiffany said hoping that he would give into her pushiness, and tell her everything that she wanted to know or at least what was the surprise.

31

Taking her by the hand and leading her out the door, "Patience my dear patience. Do you have everything you need?" Off to dinner they went, after dinner they went to hear jazz in the park. As the music played David pulled her closer to him. Perfect fit, he thought the curves of her body fell right in place with his. He turned her around and they began to dance to a slow jazz tune. "You are so beautiful." David said looking deeply into her eyes. "So beautiful." Then he leaned into her and kissed her. "Okay I think you have waited long enough, or should I say my surprise for you has waited long enough. My surprise is that I will be in town for another two weeks . . . . That right another two weeks of recruiting then back to Norfolk . . . . So can I recruit you?" David said leaning in for another kiss.

"I'm yours, where do I sign up?" Tiffany said with a smile on her face, and eyes filling up with water.

They got back in his car and started heading back toward Grandma's. "What's on your mind Tiffany, am I moving too fast for you? I only have a short time to win your heart, and that is what I am trying to do. Where another man failed you, and I want to succeed with all passing marks, I talked to my sister about you today after I left your Grandma's. She told me that I had not sounded this excited about anyone ever and that I should not just let you pass by without a fight. That is why when my Lieutenant was asking if anyone wanted to stay on for a few more weeks of recruiting, I said yes, sign me up. Who knows what I might come back to Norfolk with. I know I am moving fast, but how many times do you feel something so right and know that it is in your hands to make it come out the way you know it should be. Then you stepped up to the plate and made it happen and it turned out to be everything and more than what you ever thought. Well that is what I feel this is going to be and it is up to us to make it happen. So now can I ask you again, what's on your mind Ms Tiffany?" David said taking one hand off the steering wheel to take a hold of Tiffany's hand in her lap.

Tiffany looked up at him and said, "David you feel so right. In just the short time that we have known each other, you have made me so happy. You want to know about me, and I want to know more about you. Who am I kidding; I want to know all about you. You didn't push, and yet I just seemed to want to tell you everything. I mean everything and not hold anything back. No secrets, just all of me, and you still came back. That's real." Tiffany said with a cry in her voice. "Yes that's real."

When they finally made it back to Grandma's it was about twelve thirty. David pulled into the driveway and parked the car. "So now what, can I see you tomorrow? I got the whole day off day after tomorrow and that my lady is our day all day sun up to sun down just the two of us." David said glancing at her to see her reaction.

"Sun up to sun down, do you think you can stand being around me for that long without wanting to take me back to Grandma's? Plus I get tomorrow too. Hmm . . . I must rank pretty high on your to do list? The whole day, that sounds sweet." Tiffany said smiling from ear to ear.

David walked Tiffany to the front door and gave her a kiss, making sure not to get too passionate as he did not know how close Grandma might be and it was also pretty late. "Good night Tiffany, until tomorrow and sweet dreams of me." He said walking back to his car.

"Good night David, I will see you tomorrow." as she watched him pull away. "Good night and sweet dreams. Please God, don't let this be a dream, let him be the one, the one that I need to make me happy." She said as she went into her house. "Now little one how is this going to work with you? I guess only time will tell." as she placed her hand on her stomach and headed up the stairs.

Chapter 5

● ● ● ● ● ● ● ● ● ● ● ● ● ● ● ● ● ● ●

T wo weeks seemed to have past by so quickly and David was due to head out, back to Norfolk, back to his home and back to his life, a life without a Tiffany. No more lunches and dinners, no more slow dancing till dawn, no more walks in the parks, no more just having someone there to talk to, to hold me and not want anything more than to be with me. Just the thought made tears come down like rain as she began to cry uncontrollably.

Just then Grandma walked past her room and opened the door as she heard Tiffany crying. "What's wrong child? Are you in pain? Are you okay?" As she sat on the bed next to Tiffany to try and comfort her.

"Oh Grandma, I am such a fool. How could I let myself fall for David? Do you know in two days he is going to be gone and out of my life, back to Norfolk and the Navy? I just didn't want to face the time going by and all of the time that we spent together. Grandma am I really stupid to think that he could even begin to feel for me the way that I think I feel about him? God Grandma I am pregnant. Who wants to be in a relationship with someone who is pregnant and to top it off it's not even his kid. I'm just stupid; David was just a nice guy trying to be nice to a stupid little girl, who got herself pregnant by a man that could care less about her, just a man that wanted a trophy on his shelf, you know another notch in his belt. Well it looks like the joke is truly on me, but the only thing is, I am not laughing. Grandma what am I going to do, David will be here in thirty minutes. Should I just quit while I am ahead and when he gets here you just tell him that I am gone and just leave it at that? Grandma what am I going to do." Tiffany cried out as she held onto her grandma.

"There there baby, one thing you don't want to do is lie to this young man. You need to tell him how you're feeling and what's going on with you. Be open, be honest let him know. He has been coming around now for weeks making you smile and making sure you are happy. He needs to know the truth and he needs to hear it from you. If he is really the man that you have made him out o be, he will hear you. I mean truly hear you and know what to do. He will know what to do, I know this only because of the things that you say he has said to you, and how he has been around you and just keeps coming back to you. David is a good man; let him show you how good he is and how good he can be. Now Tiffany you just dry your eyes now and get yourself together and get dressed, he will be here for you shortly." Grandma said brushing the hair away from Tiffany's face. "Now hurry up and get yourself together."

Tiffany got up and went into the bathroom to wash her face. Let's keep it simple just a pair of shorts and a comfortable shirt and shoes, because that man loves to walk. "I know that I am right about you David. I just don't want to put so much on you. Me is one thing but adding a kid is another, and a lot to ask." Tiffany said looking in the mirror of the bathroom. Just then she heard the doorbell ring. That man is always on time she thought to herself, yes always on time. She ran out of the bathroom and into the bedroom to get dressed.

"Hello Mrs. Miller and how are you doing today?" David said as he entered the house.

"Well, David and you? Tiffany should be down in just a few minutes. You know how these young women are, they have to have everything just right before they make their entrance. You know how they want to impress you young men. So Tiffany tells me that you are only going to be in town for a few more days and you are heading back to Norfolk, Virginia? Is that right?" Grandma said looking at him with those questioning eyes.

"Yes ma'am, yes we only have a few more days here then back to Norfolk. I just hope . . . . Well I am not going to get into this right now. I really do need to talk to Tiffany. I want her to understand. Well let me stop, enough said. I mean too much said. Do you know how much longer she is going to be Mrs. Miller?" David asked rather abruptly.

"Let me just go on up here and check David. Just wait here and I will be right back." Grandma said holding onto the railing of the stair case.

"Girl don't make that man wait, he gave you a time and he is here and you should be downstairs waiting. You look fine, just beautiful now. Get out of here and remember listen to what he is saying and understand where he is at." Grandma said taking Tiffany by the hand with a firm hold. "Listen, really listen to him."

Tiffany took a deep breath and headed down the stairs. His back was to the stairs and all she could do was stair at him. Nice fitting jeans and a white polo over a body of a king. At that moment he turned and smiled as he saw her coming down the stairs.

"Tiffany you look beautiful as always." David said with a smile in his voice. "Are you ready?"

"Yes, yes I am David." Tiffany responded.

"Your chariot awaits you my queen, so that we may begin our evening." David opened the door for her and off they went.

"What's wrong Tiffany you seem nervous, are you alright?" David said patting her on the top of her leg.

"David this time has gone by so fast, too fast. You are going to be leaving in two days and you and I both know that we will never see each other again. You just don't know how you have made me feel. You have been here with me everyday laughing with me sharing with me and drying my eyes when I have cried. You have been so much to me and now you are going to be gone. David my heart is hurting I want to be with you so bad, you just don't know. No one has ever made me feel the way you have and in such a short time. David you . . . ." Tiffany began crying

"Hold on sweetheart, don't do that I . . . Wait a minute let me pull over up here and we can get out and talk or just sit in the car and talk whatever you want, just don't do that Baby." David said turning into the park entrance.

"David you are leaving? I am pregnant and everything is just happening so fast. I wish I could just make time just stop so I can think, so I can breathe. What's going to happen to when you leave? I know you don't owe me anything, and that all you were trying to do is be a good guy and show me that all guys aren't jerks and I thank you for that. Now your job is done. So thank you, because I know you have to go." Tiffany said as tears poured down her face.

"Tiffany you have to calm down, because you will not hear what I am trying to say if you don't. I have been thinking about this long and hard for the past couple of weeks and days. Like I have done about you, and I know you have also done about me. You have touched my heart like no one has ever done before. I have talked to my mom at great length about you. She really wants to meet you, the woman that I can't stop talking about, the woman I can't stop dreaming about, she really wants to meet you. Stop me if I'm moving or talking too fast. I have been thinking, and they have lots of colleges in Norfolk and if you apply now, you can go the first semester and once the baby gets here you can take a semester off then get right back into it again. So you can get your education. They have dorm rooms that have daycares in them so a mom can learn and have child care. Baby, I want you with me, I need you with me. Tell me, you don't think

I am moving too fast. I will slow down even though I don't want to, but if that is what you want I will do it, if it brings you closer to me. Military life is not easy and with you being in a dorm and me being on the base we will hardly ever see each other, but we will be in the same city and just a phone call away and trust me when you call I will be there. Tiffany please say yes, you just don't know how happy that will make me. How happy this will make us." David said pulling her closer and kissing her. "You just don't know how happy."

"School in Norfolk, Virginia, Wow! I never thought about something like that. That is so far away from everything I know, but it is a place to go to school and a chance for a new beginning and a new start. So what does this mean for us? I mean you'll be on the base and I'll be in the dorms and me going to school and you off working and traveling, recruiting. What will that mean for us, and how will we be able to just be? Then the baby will be here sooner than we know it, and I have made up my mind; I am not getting rid of my baby, see I have made up my mind about at least one thing. I need to set up an appointment to see a doctor, start taking those prenatal vitamins and doing the things I need to do for my little one. What about you, what do you want out of this, I mean this is a lot of me to ask and to want, but I really want you in my life. You feel so right, but this is a lot to ask of you. I am going to go to the Library in the morning and look up colleges in Norfolk, and start writing some letters of interest, so I can get in. I know that my grades are right and my ACT score is good enough to get into just about any school. I am going to make this happen. I want this. I am going to call my dad in the morning, because I know that he will have something to say, I just hope he will listen and understand." Tiffany said hoping that David would say something anything.

"I want you girl, you just don't know how much, but are you really ready for all of me and everything that we can be? You don't know how much I want to hold you in my arms every night, watch you sleep, and be there in the morning when you wake and just be there for you and in your life. I know you have a baby on the way, but know this. I am not a man that is going to back down from any challenge, I know too many men that do that and have done that, but I want you to know that I am not one of them. Tiffany I need you to believe that. Like I told you before, I have never felt this way about someone before. You came in my life and I don't want to go to sleep at night because that is time away from you, I can't wait until I get done with work so I can come by to see you. You just don't know Tiffany what you do to me." David said clearing his throat. "I think I am falling in love with you."

"I love you to David, I really do." Tiffany answered "My grandmother was right; she said that you were a good man and that you would say the right thing. I just hope that you, I mean that we are doing the right thing to make this work."

"That means tomorrow when I am at work; you need to be at the library getting all the information you can on the schools down there. I want you in school and able to do for yourself, because that is just as important as being together. You won't be happy if the only one you can depend on is me. Trust me I learned that from my mother. Man I can't wait for you to meet her; you will get to see for yourself how wonderful and amazing she is. We need to get you going to the doctor, because we don't want any problems with you or the baby. You both need to be happy and healthy and in my arms." David said smiling that sexy smile at her.

"Then I need to get home and get some rest because tomorrow is going to be a busy day." Tiffany said. "Yes tomorrow will be busy."

David pulls up to Grandma's house. "We have arrived, let me come around and get the door for you." David said hopping out to get the door. "Give me your hand."

"I am not some old woman. I need more than just your arm to lean on I need you" Tiffany said smiling.

David led her to the front porch and leaned in and kissed her on the lips, "Good night my love."

"Good night David, I love you." Tiffany responded. Tiffany went in the house to find Grandma sitting on the couch with the television watching her. "Grandma don't you think you need to lie down in your bed so that can get a good nights sleep? I am home now, so you don't have to worry and David is the most wonderful man I have ever met. That is next to Dad of course." as Tiffany flops down on the couch next to grandma. "It is just like you said Grandma, all I had to do was listen to David and he gave me the answers that I needed to know. Tomorrow I am going to the library and look up some colleges that are in Norfolk and see what I need to do to get in. I also need to contact my school back home and talk with a guidance counselor and have them write me a letter along with mailing my transcripts." Tiffany said barely able to contain herself.

"Looks like he is the one honey, but all the way to school in Norfolk, Virginia? Tiffany I am glad you are happy. You need this. Now when are you going to talk to your father? You know he is just going to think I just let you run wild. You need to talk to him first thing tomorrow morning, because you know he is going to want to put his two cents in. He is going to want to take all of the credit for you even coming to Memphis and finding a good man. Well you know he will take the credit after he gets done yelling about how I just let you run wild, and after he hears it in your voice about David. Be prepared to answer a million questions. If you think getting into college is going to be tough, wait till you talk to your father." Grandma said laughing as she got up from the couch and headed off to her room. "Good night sweetheart, I love you. Now you need to be getting some sleep yourself. You need your rest; you have a busy day in store for you."

"Good night Grandma, I love you to." Tiffany said holding onto one of the pillows of the couch. "Good night again to you to David."

It felt like night time had just flew by and Tiffany's alarm clock went off. She got out of bed, got in the shower, got dressed, and went down stairs. Grandma was already up and cooking breakfast as usual. "Good morning Grandma. Can I . . . ."

Before she could even finish her sentence grandma said, "The keys are on the table be careful. Before you take off you need to get something to eat and call your father. He has the right to know all of this before you set off making all of these plans."

Tiffany nervously picks up the phone to call her dad. "Good morning Michelle is my dad there? Yes everything is okay. I just have to tell him something. Something that I think he will be happy about. Well maybe not right away, but he will be happy." Tiffany said,

"Well he is in the shower right now. Hold on, I will tell him you are on the phone. Hang on okay Tiffany?" Michelle said as she sat the phone down on the counter to go and tell Ken Tiffany was on the phone for him.

"He is getting out of the shower and he'll be right down. You know all I had to say was it was you on the phone and the world stopped. You sure everything is alright?" Michelle asked in her inquisitive motherly voice.

"Okay, okay let me tell you and then maybe you can even talk to dad after he gets off of the phone with me." Tiffany replies before going on with her story about David and Norfolk to Michelle.

"Tiffany I will do what I can do on my end, but like you said you need to talk to your father. Speak of the devil here he is." Michelle says as she hands the phone over to Ken.

By the end of the conversation dads nerves were finally calming after the phone being past back and fourth from grandma to Tiffany. Before hanging up the phone dad said, "Baby I knew you were growing up and would go away to college, but I never thought college so far away. I guess I am going to have to let you grow up and see what the world is really like or you will never know for yourself. Michelle and I are planning a visit to Memphis in a couple of weeks. Don't go flying off before we get there. You understand me? Take care and I love you and tell grandma I love her too."

*　　*　　*

David's last day in Memphis came before either one of them were ready. The knowing that it would be a while before they would see each other again, it would be hard, but they would make it through until they could be together again. Between the letters and the phone calls, they would make it through.

Finally the acceptance letter arrived from college; it was to Norfolk State University. Along with another return letter from Jordan unopened and just marked return to sender. This was the third letter she had written him since she had been in Memphis, but every time the same thing happened. His loss, Tiffany thought as she placed the unopened letter in a box along with the others. He is going to know that I tried to talk, but he just never wanted to open them and read. Norfolk University, wanted Tiffany to come out and visit the campus and get registered for classes, because they would be starting up the end of August, just one month away. She could not wait to tell David the good news. Everything was really all coming together, everything, but at the same time moving so fast.

Chapter 6

● ● ● ● ● ● ● ● ● ● ● ● ● ● ● ● ● ●

Wow! This Norfolk, Virginia Tiffany thought. It has been seven weeks since she had seen David and she was ready. The phone calls were nice, but she wanted to be in his arms.

"In two more blocks, we will be at the University and your dorms." Dad said as he kept focused on the road. "Yes baby, in two more blocks and you will be in your new home. Now when is that boyfriend of yours going to show his face so that I can get a chance to meet him face-to-face instead of on the phone. You know I have to look in his eyes to see if he has the look of a good man or just a good time."

"Dad he will not be able to leave base until tomorrow morning and he has to be back by ten tomorrow night. That's okay anyway, because after ten there are no men allowed in the dorms anyway. If I need him for anything, he is only twenty minutes away from the dorms. Don't scare him off dad, I told him you were a nice man. Please daddy whatever you do, don't embarrass me." Tiffany said with that look of please daddy don't.

"Here we are. We're just going to get you all moved in and then we are going to have a nice lunch in town, if that's alright with you ladies?" Ken said looking into Michelle's eyes as if to say lets hurry up and do this and we can go to a hotel to work on the rest.

After about three hours they had Tiffany all moved in and set up to the way she wanted it. She even got the bonus of getting a really nice roommate, Shelia Turner, same taste in colors in their dorm room, good looking posters of Prince and his motorcycle and all that purple, lots of cassettes with slow jams and a snack drawer that we both would keep filled, what more could a girl ask for in a roommate. She said that she liked to keep things around her calm and quit because her mother had to get a second job to be able to send her off to college so there was no way she was going to let her down and blow it all by partying. We even shook hands on that because I told her what was going with me and that I really needed to focus as I would be here the first semester then be out for a semester then come back in the summer to catch up on what I missed for a semester, but I had to do it for myself and for my baby. As my grandma would say if you start going to school and had to quit for any reason, you need to hurry up and get back into it as soon as possible so that you wont lose all of what you are trying to achieve. "So I know I will be back after you are born little one, you just watch mommy and see." As she began to rub her belly which had grown slightly since she had last seen David. What is David going to think since there is a little bit more of me to look at, and I will just keep growing and growing and growing until finally you will be here? You are going to be a cute little New Years, January baby, then back to school for mommy in the summer. We are going to be busy. We have a doctor's appointment on Monday that Michelle and Dad want to come to. Then they will be off and running again.

Michelle seems to make him really happy. "Thank you God for looking out for him, you know he needed someone special and that is what you sent him." Tiffany said as she looked up to heaven. "Thank you."

"Young lady you have all day to look at this room, you got it in order. Now let's go look at this town a little bit and find a place to get some lunch. Then I am going to take this beautiful lady back to the hotel room and get some rest." Ken said as he smiled with that sexy smile and eyes telling Michelle that rest was really not on his mind at all.

They drove around town seeing some of the sights and ate at a little family owned restaurant, where the service and the food were great. "Dad I am getting kind of tired, I think I am ready to go back to the dorm and take a nap." Tiffany said holding her stomach.

"Are you sure you are tired and nothing else is wrong?" Ken said

"No dad I am just tired. This was a lot of work we got done today, and all of the driving and then the food. Daddy I am just tired." Tiffany said still holding her stomach.

Tiffany got back to her room and Shelia was sitting in a chair in the corner of the room knitting a blanket. "What's up girl? What are you doing?" Tiffany asked kind of chuckling at Shelia.

"Oh this? This is what I do to relax and get in the mood to take on anything these instructors can send my way. So that was your dad? He sure is handsome, and Michelle I take it that is not your mother by the way you introduced her. Well anyway she seems really nice; they both seem like good people." Shelia said just looking up every now and then from knitting.

"Yes that's my dad and no Michelle is not my mother, but she is very good people, and thanks for the compliment. The rest is a long story; we have to share stories one of these nights because it looks like we will have a lot of them ahead of us together." Tiffany said just really wanting to lie down and sleep, and that she did.

The next morning, Tiffany was so wound up, she could not wait for her dad and Michelle to get there, but most of all she wanted to see David and he would be there in about thirty minutes. Tiffany just decided that she was going to go down the hall to meet everyone as they came in. As she was sitting in the chair trying to act like she was reading a magazine she heard a voice.

"Good morning my love." David whispered in her ear. "How was the drive down? Did you get everything set in your room? If not, here I am. Whatever you need done I will help you do it." David pulled Tiffany up to give her a hug. "Oh girl, you feel so good and you look so beautiful. I can see you are poking out a little now, you still look and feel beautiful. I thought your dad would beat me here this morning. Just so that he could have the pen and paper ready for me to fill out the "Who's dating my baby girl?" form. Hell I don't blame him. I would have a guy in a sound proof box asking him question after question just to get permission to even date my daughter, and to let her move to another state. I don't know what the test would be, but it would not be easy, that's for sure. How long are your dad and Michelle going to be in Norfolk, because I was hoping that we could go by my mother's house so that you two could meet? Besides that I know my sister Karen will be at her house trying to see everything and everybody. She is so noisy. Baby, so what time is your dad going to be here? I can't wait to meet him."

"They should be here anytime. I hope you are ready for my dad, because he can be a real piece of work sometimes. Then after we sit down and talk for a while with them, then we can get in the car and drive over to your mother's house and hang out for a while. They can all meet then. My day is starting out great, I am feeling good and you are looking good. What more could a girl want?" Tiffany said holding David's hand and rocking back and forth a little. "Yes what more could a girl want?"

"A girl should want her daddy." Ken said in a deep voice coming up from behind her. "Good morning baby, and who is this young man you are dancing with without any music playing?"

"Dad this is David Morgan, he is an Aviation Electronics Technician for the Navy, and this David is my father Mr.

Kenneth Miller, but people just call him Ken or Mr. Miller if they are trying to date his daughter." Tiffany said trying to make one of them laugh or smile just to break the tension of that first meeting.

Ken broke out with a smile, "Lighten up. I don't know what my daughter has told you about me, but I know most of it is not true, even though they are still trying to locate the body of the last young man that broke her heart, but they will never find a trace of him." elbowing David as he walked by him. "No not one trace. Now David is there someplace we can go to talk privately. I have a great idea why don't you two ladies go do a little shopping and we will all meet back here about eleven. Then we will see what we'll do from there. "Ken kissed Michelle. "Now be sure to take it easy on those credit cards, you know they don't get out much with Tiffany around wanting the perfect dorm room and the expense behind that."

About eleven o'clock they all made it back. "David it looks like you survived my father. You don't have any cuts or bruises you are not showing me now are you?" Tiffany said running up to greet him.

"Baby, your dad is really cool; he wants us to go by my mother's house to meet with her and Karen. We were just waiting on you two to get back; I hope you guys have not eaten anything because Mom and Karen have been in the kitchen cooking up something special for all of us." David said looking into Tiffany's eyes.

"No we didn't. We just figured you would be showing us some restaurant that you go to or the two of you would be planning some kind of adventure for us. Your mom's house sounds wonderful." Tiffany said still grinning from ear to ear just at the thought that she and David were here and together again.

It was about a half hour drive to get to David's moms house. As they got out of the car and walked into the ranch styled home and walked into the kitchen. "Hey mom, here she is." David said as he took Tiffany by the hand leading her in front of his mom. "This is my mother, the one and only Angela Morgan and here is the one and only woman for me, Tiffany Miller."

There she was, Angela Morgan, David's mom, she stood about five nine, slender build, black long wavy hair with a complexion so deep and satiny brown chocolate, you definitely thought model when you seen her. You could definitely see who David got his looks from.

"There she is, show me some love. Hello I am Karen, David's sister"; a young lady came from out of nowhere. She stood about five seven slender build and black wavy hair, she almost looked like her mother's twin. Her wardrobe for the day was one that I knew my father would kill me if I even tried to clean the house in, she wore a tan colored tan top and some cut off blue jean shorts, that to say the least she must have done herself, and she did not leave very much fabric behind to cover anything and to top it off high heel tan sandals. She had also obviously had a little too much to drink. "Let's get this party started." as she shouted and went around and finished introducing herself to everyone.

"I am sorry. I apologize for Karen she going through a rough time right now and she . . . . well she really wanted to meet your family. Like I said I am sorry for this, she is really a super woman and does not drink that much at all. I think that is a big part of the problem with her today. I told her that things would work out, and to just give it some time." David said with a hint of embarrassment in his voice.

"Its fine David everybody goes through things, but she has a strong support system working with her to get through whatever it is she's going through." Tiffany smiled and leaned in to kiss David.

"This is another reason why I love you." David said returning the kiss.

They all sat down and ate. The conversation went on for what seemed like hours. Tiffany had started fanning herself in the Virginia heat. "Are you okay?" David asked

"Yes I'm fine, just a little hot and a lot of tired." Tiffany said fanning herself.

David took Tiffany by hand and led her in the house to cool off and rest. "So whose room is this you are taking me off to?" Tiffany asked looking around in the room. It had a queen size bed in the middle with a ocean blue quilt across it and an oak wood chest that sat at the foot of the bed and television and stereo a couple of oak dressers and a large mirror on the wall.

"This is just one of her guest rooms. Just get in the bed and lie down, take your shoes off and get comfortable. She has two, but this one is more away from all the noise in the back yard. Do you want the television on, or some quiet music playing so, you rest?" David said brushing the hair from her face. "You are so beautiful."

"I think some quiet music would be nice." Tiffany said softly.

David stood up and popped in a cassette with some jazz on it, deemed the lights until it almost looked pitch black with just a little light streaming in from under the door, locked the door, then crawled in the bed next to her and put his arm around her. "This is nice, you feel so right. This is another new first for us. Me holding you while you sleep." David whispered in her ear.

Tiffany turned in the bed facing David and they begin kissing and holding onto one another even tighter. David began moving his body in closer soon they were moving their bodies in a rhythm as if they where on a dance floor slow dancing together, Tiffany's body responding in a motion telling him that it felt right.

"Oh David." David's hand unbuttoned her blouse to grasp a hold of one of her breast as he then leaned down to kiss it. Chills ran through Tiffany's body as the moans just kept coming. She could feel him growing harder and harder as his body moved against hers, his hand ventured slowly down her legs and up her skirt. As he slid his hand into her panties he could feel her wetness and he wanted to provide her with the pleasure her body was in need of.

Just then a knock on the door. "Tiffany, honey are you alright, you looked like you weren't feeling too good outside and I just wanted to come and check on you." Angela called out from the hall before trying to open the locked door.

"Yes, yes I'm fine ma'am, I just got hot and was a little tired, but I'm feeling much better now ma'am. Thank you." Tiffany answered barely able to catch her breathe as she was trying to button up her blouse and straighten her clothes.

"David do you know that it is a little after three now, and I know you have to be back on the base by ten didn't you say? If that is the case I know you are going to want to spend some alone time with Tiffany and not just hanging out under parents the whole day." Angela questioned

"Yes mom, thank you it just looks like time is starting to get away from me." David said trying to cool his hormones down and listen for his mom to walk back down the hall. "Baby I think that we are going to have to stop for now. I think we need a little more privacy. Plus what I want to do to you will take more than a couple hours. I will need all night." David said kissing Tiffany's lips passionately again. "Let's get out of here. Are you feeling okay though?"

"Yah I'm fine. I think I have cooled down some. We are going to have to make that date happen, because I want to be warmed up by you again" Tiffany said standing up making sure her clothes were all in place before her and David walked out.

"Tiffany's feeling a little better, but I think that she needs to get back to the dorms and get some rest and I have to get back on base. So we probably need to get going." David said walking back out on the patio.

On the way back home David and Tiffany sat in the back seat looking like two little guilty kids that took something and now they have to find a way to get it back. As they sat in the back seat just exchanging glances hoping that no one else would see. Back on campus Tiffany could hardly wait to get out of the car. "See you in the morning dad and Michelle. I will call you tonight so that we can make plans for your last day here. I am just going to show David my room before he takes off for the base." Tiffany said blowing kisses in dad's direction. "Good night, love you guys."

Tiffany opened the door so that she could show David her dorm room. "Hey Shelia, have a ruff day again today, I see you over there knitting? Shelia this is my boyfriend David, and David this is my room mate Shelia. He just wanted to take a look at my room. So what do you think?" Tiffany asked with a flirty smile on her face.

"It's looks good Tiffany. So now that we have the meeting of the parents out of the way, what would you like to do for the rest of the day? Would you like to go shopping or to the movies, to the park, or just simply hang out together? Your prince is waiting for his orders." David said.

"Everything is so beautiful, but it is so hot, I will let you decide. Surprise me, my beloved prince." Tiffany said giggling. "Lead the way."

Off they went for a tour of the city. They stopped at a park and got out of the car. Walking around looking at all of the flowers, and fountains it was so breathtakingly beautiful. David started looking around as if he was trying to find something. "Tiffany sit down right here, I have something to tell you. I have been with other girls in the past but none of them have touched me the way you have. I can't do anything without thinking, "What will Tiffany think, say or do?" I love you so much. I talked with your dad today, because I knew that would be the only right thing to do. So when you and Michelle were off shopping your dad and I were talking man to man about you. I know I am doing the right thing God."

51

looking up to heaven and then in Tiffany's eyes, "Tiffany will you marry me?" David said pulling a princess cut one carat diamond, size nine gold ring out of his pocket and placed it on Tiffany's finger.

A look of pure surprise was on Tiffany's face, "Yes! Yes David I will marry you. I love you so much." she was speechless for a moment, "So my dad knows that you were going to ask me? . . . . Oh you two are so sneaky. How could he not even try to give me a hint, a clue, anything? This ring is so beautiful. David, how did you know my ring size?"

"Like I told you before your father and I have done a lot of talking together over the phone and the subject of marriage came up, and I asked him for your hand in marriage and he told me that nothing would make him happier than for us to get married. So my next question to him was what size ring does she wear? Now the rest will be our history, and I think that we are going to make a great story to tell our kids." David said almost dragging.

"One thing . . . . Can we wait till after the baby is born before we get married? I want to ask one more thing from you as well, I want for us to wait to make love until after the baby is born. I don't want to do anything that might hurt the baby or me, I mean today at your mothers house . . . . if we would have gotten started I don't think I would have been able to stop. I . . . . I don't know I just think that we should wait. I want this little one here before I say "I do" because I will be upset if I have to waddle down the isle, because I fill like I'm getting bigger by the second." Tiffany said holding her stomach and looking at David to add something to what she had just said.

"If you are looking at me to add something about what you just said you have truly lost your mind. I have been around my mother and my sister for too many years to comment on any woman's size. I think you are right; after the baby is born will be a good time to get married. Besides that, I think a spring time wedding would be nice just to see the flowers blooming all around you as you just glow down the isle. Damn Baby . . . . I can't wait to have you as my wife. And you're right today I know I would not have stopped. So after the baby is born. I got plenty of cold showers coming my way to cool down my hot need for your body." he said covering his mouth and laughing. "I know you will be worth any and everything that I have to wait for." he kissed her lips and leaned back and bit his bottom lip. "Now kissing to still aloud, right?"

Chapter 7

● ● ● ● ● ● ● ● ● ● ● ● ● ● ● ● ● ● ●

The first semester was finally over and Tiffany was glad, with the baby always kicking and moving it was hard to study with a full load of classes. She was also kind of sad and happy at the same time knowing that she would not be back until summer, but when she came back she would be a mother and a wife. David was coming over to help her move her things out of the dorms and into an apartment a few blocks away from the naval base. Dad said that he would fit the bill this time or at least for the first six months. Why did it have to be January she thought it seems so cold. She was also glad the furniture company had already moved in a lot of her things, so what she had in the dorm room was easy to get moved out.

David pulled up along with some of his friends, "Tiffany you look tired, are you feeling okay? Why don't you just go on and drive my car over to your apartment and just rest, the bed and everything has already been set up, so just go and get comfortable." David said handing her keys to his car.

"I'll be fine; the baby has just been really sitting in a bad position today. Maybe he knows its moving day, and he wants to do his part. I'll go and just lay down like you said." Tiffany said waddled off to the car. "See you soon."

David and his friends got everything loaded onto the truck in about an hour, and then into the apartment. Tiffany looked at David when he came into the bedroom and said, "David, I think its time." with a look of sheer panic on her face. Off to the hospital they went and about four hours later Kendall Michael Morgan was born, seven pounds eight ounces and twenty one inches long. Two days later both mom and baby got to go home to their new apartment.

* * *

April twenty ninth Tiffany and David were married, Tiffany in a beautiful long fitted white gown and David in his Navel uniform. It was a picture perfect scene with friends and family there wishing them well. The honeymoon was next, off to Cancun for a week. Ken and Michelle took Kendall back home with them, so that David and Tiffany would have no worries, just good times. They arrived in Cancun one day later, for the first time in four months no baby, no work just each other, they both had wanted this time alone together for so long it seemed. They went to the hotel and relaxed for a while, then got dressed for dinner. Tiffany wore a stunning red halter dress that with every turn and bend she took seemed to caress her body, never wearing too much makeup, why with beauty like that who needed it.

David looking like the perfect gentlemen had on black pants with a tropical red print button down short sleeve shirt, that he had left just enough buttons unbuttoned to show Tiffany what she would be holding onto for the rest of their lives together. As they ate they listened to island music and after they finished dinner they danced, they got back to their room to find a bottle of wine on their bed and a card that said "CONGRATULATIONS!"

Tiffany sat down on the bed and reached for her night gown, and went into the bathroom to change. David poured two glasses of wine. "Congratulations Mrs. Morgan" David said holding out a glass for her to toast with.

"Congratulations to you to Mr. Morgan." Tiffany smiled sitting on the bed in her white satin almost floor length gown.

David got up from the bed and lit some of the candles that had been arranged around the bed, he turned to Tiffany took her by the hand, "Can I have this dance?" He said pulling her closer to him. They danced around to music only the two of them heard in their minds then stood still and started kissing. "We are married now and we can do this anytime or any place, and no one can say anything, because we are married, isn't that right Mrs. Morgan?" as he returned to kissing her and holding her close. "Now we can do this officially." then he reached behind her and untied the strings to her night gown, then he began kissing her shoulder and neck. Tiffany closed her eyes and tilted her head so that all access was given to him. His hand cupped her breast as he began to wrap his lips around them, as moans came from her as the feeling of passion were running through her like crazy. In one scoop he picked her up and moved her over to the bed as her gown fell to the floor, he laid her across the bed and began rubbing the inside of her thighs, she responded by opening them wider to allow better access for whatever he had planned, she could feel his tongue entering her, she grabbed a hold of his head pulling him deeper inside her, calling out his name and moaning was all she could do to respond what he was doing and all David wanted to hear. He waited until he not only could feel the sweat all over her body but could taste the satisfaction coming out of her as well.

He stood up and undid his belt and let his pants fall to the floor, he was already standing at attention and pointing in her direction and ready to go. Tiffany sat up in bed and moved toward the edge of the bed and took him in her mouth enjoying him better than she enjoyed any ice cream cone, she had ever eaten. "Oh Baby that feels so good, don't stop." David cried "Oh please don't stop." He pulled back as he wanted to be inside of her when he released himself. "You are going to enjoy all of me tonight; you don't know how bad

I want this. You don't know how bad I want you." As he lay down on top her and slowly entered inside her, with every push Tiffany held onto David tighter. David reached under her and turned her body on top of his so that she could enjoy the ride from on top, he then released himself inside of her. Their bodies covered in sweat and satisfaction fell asleep in each others arms.

The week long honeymoon ended as fast as it began. "Come on Baby hurry up or we are going to miss our plane, and I have to get back to work and we have to get back to Kendall. You know your Dad and Michelle are not ready to be parents to a new born all over of again, so lets get back so we can give them a break." David said.

"Don't rush me. After a week of all of that, you think it is easy to walk?" Tiffany said smiling.

The plane finally landed and they were home. "Home sweet home." Tiffany said walking into the airport. "I never thought that I would be this happy to ever get back home, but I am ready. Ready to go back to school, ready to get our base house in order, ready for my baby to be back home, I am just ready."

"Calm down Baby we have the rest of our lives together, so slow down and just enjoy. Kendall will be home in a few days and driving you and me crazy. You will be starting school in a few months. Baby I know you are ready to go, but just slow down for a second and breathe. When you calm down and relaxed a little later you can enjoy some more of me, Mrs. Morgan." David said with that flirty smile of his on his face.

"Well I will just have to do that then, because I can't let my husband down now. Can I?" Tiffany said as she switched past in a hurry to get home and life started as a real family.

After they had got back to their house, they were too tired to even unpack never the less make love. They both just fell across the bed clothes on and just slept.

Chapter 8

● ● ● ● ● ● ● ● ● ● ● ● ● ● ● ● ● ● ●

"Happy Anniversary Baby! I can't believe we have been together for thirteen years. Three beautiful children and I still want some more. We lived overseas in Japan for our first two years of marriage, and returning home and bought our first house and now we are ready to buy our dream house the one that I had my eyes on for years. Are you sure that we can afford it. I know I keep asking, but it is so beautiful, I just want to pinch myself and tell myself that I am not dreaming. Then me getting my bachelors degree in Accounting seven years ago took my CPA exam and passed the first time and now I am a CPA and making pretty good money doing it, and you an Electronics Technician for the civilian side of things and they can't get enough of you." Tiffany said, sitting down on the bed beside David as he slowly opened up his eyes to see her smiling face.

"Good morning and happy anniversary to you to. What are we going to do today to celebrate? I know our favorite restaurant will be expecting us about six this evening. Oh and if you are a good girl after dinner I think I have a little surprise for you, but only if you are good. I know the kids are planning a little surprise for us as well. So act surprised. Tiffany I know we have been through a lot and we still have a lot of things to go through. I know that we have had our ups and downs, but we stuck it out and that's what it takes for couples these days. What am I talking about that is what it takes for marriages to work these days? Like when Jordan called after five years and wanted to start playing dad and he wanted you to bring Kendall to him and I could not take off work and you went by yourself, and you stayed there for two weeks. The only thing I wanted to do when the two of you got back was to just hold the both of you and not let go. Then all the phone calls that you had take from Jordan so the two of you could work things out. I know it hurt you when you found out that I had an affair or should I say a one night stand that turned into a life long child support payment with a woman in New York and the bitch doesn't want me to have anything to do the kid but just pay the support. That's a damn shame because if I saw that kid on the street today I would not even know her. All I know is that she is a girl and should be about nine now. Man what was I thinking? This is the kind of stuff that happens that lets me know that I married the right woman and that I truly love you." Just then he pulled Tiffany down on top of him and they began kissing.

"Close the door!" the children yelled in from out in the hall. Then in came Kendall thirteen, Jessica ten and Anna eight.

"Surprise mom and dad we made you breakfast for your anniversary today and we also got you guys a present to." Little Anna said pushing her way through her brother and sister. "Yep and I picked it out all by myself, they just helped pay for it" She said rolling her eyes back at Kendall and Jessica.

Tiffany took the gift from Anna and gave her a kiss on the forehead, "Thank you, my littlest princess." She then began to open it. "Oh, I can't wait." She tore open the paper and there it was matching blue silk pajamas. "This is perfect, I love it. You kids are the best, I love you all." as she reached out to hug them all at once.

"This is great, now me and your mom can sit on the couch all hours of the night watching movies and match. No seriously I love them, they are my favorite color and they will make your mommy feel real nice in daddy's arms." David said grabbing onto Tiffany. "Now we all need to get up and get dressed and start our day. Tiffany, I need to go by the job site for about an hour and then I am yours for the rest of the day. I'm just going to ride my motorcycle over there so they won't try to keep me.'

"David, but it's . . . ." Tiffany started to talk before David cut her off with a kiss.

"One hour I promise. I will even give you your gift when I return. Baby please don't be mad, remember we have to pay for this dream house. Our dream house, so baby please, just give me one hour, just one." He said putting on his glasses and grabbing his keys.

Tiffany got up and went into the shower and came out to find in the middle of the bed was a tropical green sundress with large island flowers all over it that David had laid out for her to wear, with a note on it. "Put this on before I get back and your anniversary island adventure will begin, and always remember I love you. Hope you like the dress Anna and Jessica helped me pick it out for you." Tiffany laughed as she read it. She sat down in front of the mirror after getting dressed and started curling her hair as she smiled at herself in the mirror, and thought how truly blessed she was to have such a wonderful family and beautiful house. David where are you it has been more than an hour she thought. This is just not like him, not like him at all. I am not going to call, I am going to wait patiently and he'll be here soon, I know it. Patience she thought, Angela had already came and got the kids as they were spending the weekend with her, now I am just sitting here alone. Where could he be?

Thirty minutes later a dark blue car pulled up in the driveway. They must be lost or something. Who are these men? The doorbell rang. "Are you Mrs. David Morgan?" one of the men asked.

"Yes, yes I am. How can I help you?" Tiffany questioned the men.

"Ma'am there has been an accident and your husband has been taken to the hospital. We don't know the extent of his injuries, but if you would come with us we can get you there safely?" The first man said removing the sun glasses from his face and looking at Tiffany.

"This can't be happening it's our Anniversary we are supposed to be going out to dinner. This is a joke, you guys are joking. You need to call David and tell him this is the worse joke ever. You two need to stop. Tell him, he can get out of the back seat now. David come on now! David the joke is over!" as a strange feeling started to take over her. "Okay so please tell me again you are taking me to what restaurant, because I know you are not taking me to the hospital, because my husband knows how to ride that motorcycle and he told me that he would only be gone an hour." as Tiffany began to break down.

One of the men took her by the hand, "Ma'am I think we need to get out of here and get you up there to see him." He started leading her to the back seat of the car. "Do you need to grab your purse or anything before we get out of here?"

About a mile down the street, she looked out the window to see a tow truck driver cleaning up the street and David's mangled motorcycle, and blood, there was so much blood on the street. "You said my husband is okay didn't you? Why is there so much blood everywhere? You need to drive faster. David I'm on my way." Tiffany said as her heart began to beat uneasily and her stomach began to tighten.

As soon as the car stopped Tiffany jumped out and ran into the hospital. "Where is he? I am looking for my husband David Morgan; they said that he was in an accident. I just need to know where he's at and that he's okay and I can take him home with me." Tiffany called out to the nurse at the

ER counter. "Did you hear me, I need my husband, David Morgan! Where is he? I need him now!"

A nurse came from behind the desk. "Honey your husband is right back there, but you need to calm down. We need to talk to you first." The nurse said as she put her arm around Tiffany with a firm grip. "Now come on over here and have a seat." She pushed a call button. "Could you let Dr. Jackson know that Mrs. Morgan is here now."

"What? Why do I need to see a doctor? Why can't I see my husband? Where is he? I want to see him now, right now!" as she stood up and began to frantically walk down the hallway.

Just then a large white man walked up to her. "Mrs. Morgan, I really wanted us to talk in a private room before we go in to see your husband. I'm sorry, the impact from the truck was too great and David's injuries too extensive. I'm sorry Mrs. Morgan there was nothing we could do to save him."

* * *

A week later was the funeral, and Tiffany still unable to talk to anyone. Michelle and Karen helped to dress her for the service. The church was calm and quiet, the smell of magnolia blossoms filled the air of the church, the casket was closed, four large pictures of David were placed around the casket for the mourners to view. At the cemetery after the firing of the guns, playing of taps and being handed the folded American flag from David's casket, she was numb. The kids tried to be there to comfort her but to no avail. Karen and Ken talked and thought that it would be best if Tiffany and kids went to with Ken for a while or at least until she got herself back on her feet again.

After being off work for a week and not really talking with anyone Tiffany went down stairs and into the kitchen where Ken and Michelle were sitting at the table enjoying a cup of coffee. "I have to get the house in order and my job; they are going to want me there Monday morning. I've had enough time off. I've got to get back to living again. Dad you can take the kids I just need a little more time. Then I'll come out to visit and pick them up in a few weeks." She looked at the cards on the table and started to go through them to see who sent them. "I need to read all of these cards and condolences that everyone has sent. I looked through them, and Jordan sent me one." Tiffany paused and looked up at her dad. "I think that would be good for them. They need to get away, and what better place than with you and Michelle. I'll just stay back, take a few days and just breathe and get my head together. I have not stopped since that day. I just won't let myself stop, because if I do it just repeats again, and I can't stand it!" Tiffany said holding herself and rubbing up and down on her arms.

"You're going to make it through this; it's just going to take some time. Jordan is not a bad a man, he was a stupid boy, but not a bad man at all. I know that he will enjoy spending some time with Kendall and helping work through this. You are a fighter and you can weather any storm that comes your way. Just pray and ask God for what you need. He'll know just what to give you." Ken said holding his baby girl. "He'll give it to you, you just wait and see."

Ken went into the other room with the kids, telling them that they were going to stay with him and Michelle for a while, and soon their mother would be there to get them. They just needed to give her a little time. The next morning they were off and gone before ten. "Bye mom we all love you and hurry up and come be with us, because we are going to miss you." Jessica said looking ticked off that she had to even go.

"Bye mom love you too, take care and call me if you want to talk, because trust me I will be calling you." Kendall said wrapping his arms around his mom trying to hold back the tears.

"Love you mommy! I am going to miss you. Hurry and come get us." Anna said climbing into the back seat of Ken's car holding onto her teddy bear. "Baby bear says he loves you too, and he will stay here to keep you company at night, if you need him to."

"I love you guys too, and I will be there to get you sooner than you think. Anna you hang onto Baby Bear and let him sleep with you, to keep you company at night." Tiffany said blowing kisses at the van as Ken backed out the driveway and drove off.

Tiffany spent many nights and weeks just being alone and working. Just trying to do things to keep her mind off her life and about what her focus should be on. In fact seven weeks had gone by without her even talking with her children. Ken had left her several messages to return his call or else he would come down and find out for himself what was happening with her. Ken had even called Karen, to have her stop by and check her and find if and what she might need. He really just wanted someone that he could trust close by to check on his baby girl.

Karen went by as often as she could and hung out for hours and sometimes would even spend the night just so Tiffany would not be alone. She couldn't imagine how hurt and alone she must feel with the loss of a man like David. Karen knew that Tiffany would finally have to start packing all of David's things and she wanted to be there to support her. Tiffany would come home and just sit up watching television until she would fall asleep on the couch. The only way she would go into her room was to get clothes out to wear; she just did not want to be in there without David coming home to be with her.

Four months had gone by and Tiffany had made up her mind that she was moving back home. The kids were already there and signed up and back in school all they needed was their mother there to get their lives back in order. Since after David's death the house was paid for, all she would have to do now is get it sold. She put her house on the market. She knew she wanted to move back home, even though home hadn't been home for thirteen years that is where she wanted to be. She called a real estate agent to send her photos and information of some homes in the area. She was ready to make this move, enough time had past already.

By October she had found a house, and her house was sold now she was ready to get packed and move. Tiffany slowly opened the door to her bedroom, her heart started racing. I can get through this; I know I can, she thought to herself. She opened David's closet and with a deep breath began putting his clothes in boxes. It really all seemed so final now, as she reached in the back of the closet, she found a large package. Tiffany pulled it out to open it. It was the anniversary gift that David had gotten her, it was a painting of her leaning against the rail of a yacht as her hair blew in the wind, David had always said that this was one of his favorite pictures of her, and the way he wanted to remember her and that moment. Tears started to run down her face. "I have to finish this. It needs to be over with." Tiffany said aloud. "I love you David, always and forever."

Angela and Karen along with some of David and Tiffany's friends came over to help her get everything in order. By the end of the night Tiffany found herself smiling and laughing, something she had not done in so long and it felt good. "I am going to miss you guys, but I will be back to visit. Angela and Karen you know I will be back with the kids to visit you guys. I know that I can always come back if I want to, you're my second family. You guys have all been there for me, and I want to thank you all. This is what family and friendship is all about. Thank you." Tiffany said starting to choke up on her words. "Looks like we got everything out and in the truck, so I guess that means I am going to get to spend my last night hanging out with you Angela, what do you think about that?" Tiffany said with a smile.

"Do you even have to ask, my daughter-in-law is leaving town and I don't know when I will see you again, you think that your last night is going to be spent in some hotel room? We are going to spend the whole night together just laughing. I don't want to see another tear of sadness fall from those beautiful brown eyes." Angela said smiling her motherly smile. "And we even might have Karen come over to laugh with us before you leave out in the morning. I just wish there was something that I could do or say to make you change your mind about leaving."

It was an early night as Tiffany knew it was going to be a long drive back home and she was driving it all alone. She got up the next morning and said her good byes to Angela and told her that she would be back with the kids to visit all of the time, because they needed their grandmother and that she needed her to.

By night fall she was back in her home town, tired and ready to lay down. She pulled up in front of her dad's house and got out. Tiffany opened up the door "Hey everyone I'm here. Where are you all at?" Tiffany said as she peeked around the corner into the front room. There they all were in front of the television. The kids jumped up and ran over to Tiffany.

"Mommy, we missed you so much! You are never going to stay away from us this long again!" Anna said leaping into Tiffany's arms

"Hey mom, what took you so long? We thought you would be here about three o'clock." Kendall said hugging Tiffany.

"I love you mom." Was all Jessica could manage to even say before the tears started to flow.

"Oh babies I'm here and we are together and I'm not going anywhere. I've been away from you guys way too long and missed out on too much already. Your mom is not going anywhere, but to sleep." Tiffany said hugging her babies "Tomorrow will move that big truck over to our new house and start unpacking."

Chapter 9

● ● ● ● ● ● ● ● ● ● ● ● ● ● ● ● ● ●

"**Y**ou can't just avoid going to church, you have been back for a month and have not stepped foot in the church. If you are not going because of Jordan, he won't bite you; he has grown up and matured a lot. He does a lot of work with the young people in the church, and he and Kendall spend quite a bit of time together. He is a changed man, he has his own business, and is doing quite well, I hear. He and Brooklyn are no longer together, I don't think they stayed together for very long anyway, the two of them just never really clicked, but that's in the past. Go on, go to church, and see for yourself, and while you're there enjoy some church to." Ken said to Tiffany over the phone.

"You're right Dad I do need to get back into church. I am just not ready for all of the, I'm sorry for your loss and if there is anything I can dos. Dad I am just not ready. Let me get past Thanksgiving and I'll be ready."

"Why should God have to wait for you? Have you ever had to wait on Him?" Ken asked.

"Okay dad okay. I'll do it. I'll go."

"Thanksgiving is at the house so don't worry about cooking anything, just bring you and the kids."

Thanksgiving Day and Tiffany and the kids headed to Ken and Michelle's. They were all in the front room when the doorbell rang. Tiffany got up to answer the door, and who of all people but Jordan stood there with a German chocolate cake in his hands. "So do I get to come in, or do I just have to stand outside holding this and wait?"

"I'm sorry, come in." Tiffany said as she moved aside to allow him in. She took the cake from his hands.

"So how have you been Tiffany?" Jordan said smugly.

"I've been hanging in there and you? I hear things have been going well for you?"

"Oh you've been asking?" Jordan responded with a cocky grin on his face.

"I haven't been asking, but everyone seems to want me to know."

The rest of the evening went by fairly quickly with more friends coming by playing card games and watching football on TV. Tiffany went upstairs to her old bedroom and laid down and went to sleep. Before long she heard a knock the door. "Come in." She sat up.

Jordan came in the door, "Hey Tiffany do you mind if I come in?"

"Sure come in, have a seat." She said as she moved her legs over in the bed so Jordan could sit down.

"So how have you really been Tiff?"

"I've been hanging in there. You know working and taking care of my kids."

"You've been doing a great job with them I might add."

Jordan started looking around the room. "Man does this room bring back memories."

"Yeah, it's the past, and behind us like it should be." Looking him in his eyes.

"I needed that, I guess. So what can I do to show that I have grown up and I'm not that same old little teenage boy anymore?"

"Oh that little teenage boy that returned all my letters return to sender?"

"What letters, I never got any letters from you until after you where married and Kendall was walking and talking. I had no idea where the two you where, and your dad wasn't saying nothing."

"What do you mean the week I left I wrote you a letter when I was staying with my grandma, and you returned it. I still have all the letters if you want to see them?"

"Why have you saved them after all this time? What you were hoping one day, maybe?"

"You know your cockiness is still so unreal."

"No . . . . stop, Lets start this again. I'm sorry for yesterday a thousand times over, but I never got any mail from you."

"It was probably your mom. You know she never did like me, and to think that I was pregnant. She probably thought I was trying to trap her all-star son. Please, did I look like Brooklyn to her?"

"No thank God for that, the two of you are nothing alike. I'm just going to apologize for all of that that happened back then. Like I said before I would like to show you that I'm not a teenage boy anymore."

"What are you trying to do, get a date with me?"

"Get date or just a little bit of time with you. What can I do?"

Tiffany got out the bed and stood up and walked over to Jordan and stood in front of him. "Right now I have time for me and my kids, and that's enough for me right now."

Jordan stood up and leaned down and softly kissed her on the lips. "I'll take that as hope, and as long as there's hope, I stand a chance." Then he turned and walked out.

All Tiffany could do was touch the lips that Jordan just kissed and she sighed.

*　　*　　*

Sunday morning rolled around again and Tiffany called her dad to talk. "When the kids get back from church, I guess we will start decorating for Christmas, and I will think about church next Sunday. Love you Dad, see you when you come pick up the kids for church." Tiffany said quickly hanging up the phone so that Ken would not keep pushing the issue of church.

After church Kendall came in the house and went up to Tiffany "Mom, Ms. Brenda wanted me to give you an invitation to her wedding next Saturday and to the reception following. Are you going to go mom? Think of it this way, it will be a few people from the church, laugh and just say "Hi! And Good bye", and be done with it. Come on mom you should go. You don't do anything but go to work, come home, and go over to granddads house. You need a social life . . . . Bad!" Kendall said smiling at Tiffany

"You win I will go. You and your sisters will have to help me pick out something nice to wear." Tiffany said throwing her hands in the air.

"Not only that, but my Dads gonna be there too. He just wants to see and make sure that you're truly okay, and . . . . Well he just asked about you that's all." Kendall said with a sly smile on his face.

"Jordan is going to be there? Well it looks like I am just going to have to find someone to go with. I just don't like feeling I'm being put on the market for dating or match making. It's just too soon. If Jordan is Jordan, then I'm sure he will be his flirting and scheming self, and we all know where that is going to go." Tiffany said with a hint of frustration in her voice. "That's it! I will just find someone to go with me. I know this guy that I work with who has been asking me out. Maybe I will just ask him."

"Mom give Dad a chance, he has changed and he's been asking about you." Kendall said, "I think he still likes you mom. One little date, what could that hurt?"

In Tiffany's mind she thought. One little date can cause a lot of unwanted pain, and I really don't want to go through all of that again. He's not changed that much. "Look Kendall

I will talk to him on the phone, but a date is just not going to happen. Not now not even in the future. Don't get me wrong I'm sure he is a good guy and he has been there for you, but I'm just not ready. Not ready for him or anyone else. I'm just happy dating me, myself and I, that doesn't hurt. He can be my friend. That's all I need from Jordan." Tiffany said putting her arm around Kendall.

"Oh you said friends, so there's hope?" Kendall said

"Come on Jessica we can pick the dress out for mom. You know if we let her do it, she will be wearing a pair of jeans and a sweater, and will be sitting in a corner looking bored and being a square. We have to make mom look hot, and get her back out there and not looking like a nerd. Let's go to mom's room to see what she is hiding in her closet." Kendall said as he took Jessica by the hand and pulled her down the hall to Tiffany's room.

"Kendall let go, I can walk!" Jessica yells and pulls away from Kendall and ran down the hall to Tiffany's room in front of him.

Tiffany thought to herself, I know I'm in trouble with those two working on something for me to wear. I hope I'll be able to walk into a church for the wedding with what they'll come up with. She walked down the hall, she past by the painting that David had made for their anniversary of her leaning against the rail with her hair blowing in the wind. "David what do you think I should do? Baby what am I going to do without you? You were right I was so happy in this picture, because you were there and everything was right. You are gone now and I'm so alone and I feel so lost. Help me, please help me." she whispered and reached her hand out to touch the painting. She walked in her room to find Kendall and Jessica pulling out dress after dress in the hopes to find the right one. "You guys just want to spare me the cleanup, and we could just go to the mall, to find something? Along with all of the Christmas traffic, I guess the mall will be as good of a place if any to start. Put all of my dresses back, and hurry up before I change my mind, and on the way back we will stop by and pick up Anna from your granddad's house."

They got in the car and were driving down the street, "Hey mom, there it is, Dads store, Jordan's Lawn Care and Landscaping Shop. You know he is good because even in the winter his doors are still open for business. See, he does snow removal. He even does the older people at the churches snow removal for free. We need a Christmas tree and guess what mom? He sells them to. Let's say we get one today after we come from the mall? He said when I'm old enough he will let me work for him and have my own crew to work with me. You know I think he could use a new accountant. You know any good ones?" Kendall said looking starry eyed at his mom. "Can we stop back by and get a tree?"

"Kendall that is enough we came out here to find a new dress for me, then to pick your sister up. Not get a Christmas tree, besides I think your grandfather is going to pick one up next weekend. Enough is enough!" Tiffany said rather agitated.

After five stores they were done and out the door to pick up Anna. "Hey Dad, hey Michelle where's Anna? You two go find your sister. Are you still planning to get the kids a tree next week? They were just asking me about one on the way to the mall today, and also showing Jordan's shop and the fact that he sells trees and that we should have picked one up. Kendall is really pushing his father, but I am just not ready to make that move. It just seems like yesterday David was right here, and I just don't want to let go, you know dad it's hard. This will be my first Christmas in fourteen years without him; Thanksgiving was hard enough I just stayed in my room and cried the whole night until I fell asleep after I left your house. Does it truly ever get easier dad? I mean you and mom were to me the perfect couple, then the next minute she's gone, and you were left with no one to laugh with, talk to, and fuss with, share secrets with, all of it gone without even giving you a chance to prepare yourself for a loss. I mean dad, David and I had it all, good kids, good jobs and we had found the perfect home, furnished and decorated it and got the yard together just the way I wanted. Thirteen years of marriage, how can you just turn off thirteen years like it didn't mean anything then just move on to the next one in line like yesterday never happened. You were so lucky to find Michelle. The two of you got together and moved almost as fast as David and me getting married, now look at the two of you ten years, and you seem to be as happy as you were when I first saw the two of you together. That's what I want, but I'm just so scared of being hurt or being heart broken again, now I have not just one, but three kids to think about. Daddy I just need your help on this one, everything is just happening so fast and I still have not even taken my ring off my finger, because if I take it off, then it will really be true, that David is dead and won't be coming through the door to pick me and the kids up ever again." Looking at the back door to see if it would open and David would be there.

"Baby there is no set way to know when the right person will come along, but at the same time you just can't keep locking yourself away from everyone either. You can't let the hurt you are feeling destroy the rest of your life. You will know when the time is right and when the right person comes along. Follow your heart. You start by making a list of what you really want in a relationship, then a list of the things that you will put up with in a relationship and finally a list of things that will break the deal of any chance of a real relationship. Be willing to have him do the same, so you both go in with open and honest eyes knowing the truth and telling the truth. Start in the beginning so you don't have to play those little I'm sorry, I didn't know games in the end. I know it sounds crazy, but it works. The hard part is the deal breaker list, many of us have one but we tend to over look the deal breakers when our hearts are feeling a little scared and a little unsure if that the other person will understand, we think we might lose something, but then we end up hating and hurting one another. Not to change the subject, but I am going to get a tree for the house this weekend and bring it by to set up. So are you going to go to Brenda's wedding next Saturday? I noticed that she gave an invitation to Kendall to give to you. You got a date or are you going solo? I can set you up with someone, if you need some help?" Nudging her on the shoulder.

"You can just bring the tree by any time next weekend, I will be kind of in and out, but the kids will be there. And, yes I am going to the wedding, the kids and I picked out a dress and some shoes for me to wear from the mall today, and I was thinking about asking this guy that I work with. His name is Bill he is a little bit younger than me and, he's new to the area and doesn't really know anyone yet. He has asked me out for drinks a couple of times, but I always came up with an excuse of why I couldn't, plus the bar and club thing is really not me. So I'll just have to see what he says." kind of shrugging her shoulders.

"Make that list when you go home when you have some quiet time to yourself. Don't go jumping into a lake you can't swim in. You might drown." Kissing her on the cheeks as the children came running in.

"Get your coats on and let's go. Love you guys, and I will make those lists tonight and I'll follow them to." closing the door behind herself.

Now at home settling down, "Dinner will be ready in a few minutes. Make sure that you have your clothes picked out for school in the morning and make sure your homework is done . . . I mean it!" Stirring the pot of chili, as the smell ran through the house calling the children down stairs and into the kitchen.

"Come in and have a seat and get ready to eat the best chili ever made. After that a movie or homework whatever you have to do, then a shower or bath and to bed. So we can all get a good night sleep, because I have a busy day at work tomorrow."

Watching the movie her mind kept drifting off to the lists that she wanted to make and could she really follow them. After the movie the kids went up stairs to take showers and to get ready for bed. "Good night mom we love you." they all said in unison.

"Good night, I love all of you to." yelling up the stairs with a smile of love written all over her face. She gathered up her blanket and headed down the hall to her room, went in the room got dressed for bed, and sat on the bed with a notebook and pen and began to write.

Things that I really want in a relationship . . . .

1. Real love
2. Someone that truly loves my children.
3. Someone that I can talk to, not just make love to.
4. Someone who is real, and that will tell me the truth even it hurts.
5. Someone who wants me and only me. I don't want to be the other woman, just another woman or a bed warmer.
6. Someone that is in the church and believes in God.
7. Someone that wants something more out of a relationship then just to be a boyfriend. We are both too old for that stuff.
8. Someone who really knows and respects my worth.

Things that I will not put up with in a relationship . . . .

1. Secrets
2. Drug use.
3. Lying to me. Tell me the truth even it hurts. Let me know from you not from someone in the streets.
4. Being in a relationship with me plus more, or if he is married.
5. Honesty! Honesty! Honesty!

6. Having sex with anyone other than me.
7. If he is already in a relationship let him work things out with her. If he can't be faithful to her what chance do I have with his loyalty to me?

Enough she thought and finished and folded the letter and put it in her purse. "I'm going to get through this and get on with my life." She thought looking down at the ring on her finger. "Oh David I love you and I miss you." laying her head down on her pillow and put her finger on her lips. Thoughts went to Jordan and the kiss he gave her on Thanksgiving. "Jordan don't do this to me again, because I can still feel your lips kissing mine." She reached over and turned off her light.

Six o'clock and the alarm clock began ringing. "Oh no, I don't feel like working today." She threw the covers off her, jumped in the shower then got dressed.

Soon she heard the kids coming down the stairs. "Mom you look nice today. When did you get that suit you look all professional and about business." Kendall said circling around his mom.

"I wear a suit everyday to work what are you talking about?"

"Mom in that suit the way it's fitting you mean business. I just don't know what kind. Are you going to ask that man that you work with to be your date at the wedding? How much do you know about him anyway, he could be a creep? Can you bring him by here first? So that we can check him out, and find out what he's about?"

"I know enough and get out of this grown persons business, eat something and finish getting ready for school. Your bus will be here soon, I'm gone, I'll see you guys when I get home this evening." Tiffany said rushing out the door so that she would not be late.

She drove to work and parked then looked in the rear view mirror to check her hair and make up before she walked in.

She walked by Bill's office which he had the door open and was looking through a file on his desk. "Good morning Bill. How was your weekend?"

"It was alright in this square town ain't like you are going to get in much trouble. What about you? How was your weekend? Miss me? You know I'm only a phone call away? I really think we would be good together if you'd just give a chance you would see. All I need is just one chance."

"Okay Mr. Give Me A Chance, how about going to a wedding and reception, that I was invited to on Saturday, then maybe go out for a little while after that?"

"Now you're not trying to marry a brother, because I'm not ready to go down that road anytime soon? Cause I know how you girls get at weddings, all starry eyed and crying that, "Oh I wish that was us." and the "Oh everything looks so beautiful. Don't you just want to? The marriage thing, No! But taking you there and then going out later? Now that would be my pleasure."

"I just didn't want to go by myself and look out of place just sitting there."

"Sure why not? Give me your address and I'll swing by and pick you up, and we can just hang out, Sound cool? What time do I need to come by and pick you up for our hot date this weekend?"

"I am thinking about 12:30, the wedding starts at 1:00, but I would like to be there a little early so that we can get a good seat. The church is about ten minutes away from my house. Thanks for agreeing to go with me, I really appreciate it. So what do you want to do afterwards? I have not been out in this town since I moved back, but it all looks the same. You know same people same places."

"I don't know yet, just some place to really show you off, and if you wear an outfit like the way that one is fitting you today. We'll be in there." Bill said shaking his head up and down and rubbing his chin.

"It is just a suit and I wear one everyday to work, what's the big deal?"

*   *   *

Saturday arrived almost over night. She peeked out her window when she heard a truck pull up in front of her house; it was her dad and Jordan with the Christmas tree. "Oh great, I'm going to kill you Dad for this one. Why Jordan? Why today?" she mumbled to herself opening up the door wearing her light blue fuzzy flannel pajamas. "Good morning everyone, Dad I thought that you would call first? And how are you doing Jordan long time no see." as she tried to brush her hair back with her fingers. "Thanks for everything that you have been doing with Kendall. He really likes hanging out with you." thinking to herself, age had done his body good, I mean real good. She had to stop herself from looking and regain her focus. "So where are you going to set up the tree at? I was thinking over there right in front of the bay window. I think that would be nice. Have you guys eaten anything yet? Let me go back here and get dressed and I'll fix you all something to eat. Sound good? I'm sure the kids will be down here in no time since I'm sure they were looking out the window and saw you pull up." Tiffany went to her room and threw on some clothes and came back and cooked breakfast. They sat and laughed and talked for a little bit, and she found herself drawn to his lips as he drank his coffee with the steam drafting off into his mustache and the cream from the coffee left a little spot on his mustache that she just wanted to lick off, then his tongue went over his lips as he looked in her direction and winked after he finished his drink. "Oh let me get you a napkin." Then she looked up at the clock. "I did not realize that the time was going by so fast, it's almost eleven o'clock and I need to start getting ready for this wedding and Bill will be here soon to pick me up. Thank you once again for the tree. It's nice."

As she was walking past Jordan, he reached out to her, "Tiffany we need to talk, I mean one on one sit down and really talk. I know not right now but soon I hope. I'll see you at the wedding to, and I guess meet your new fella I just hope he knows your worth, I just wish I would not have waited so long to know your worth. You know you still look so beautiful and your smile is so sweet. I'll see you later. Oh and thanks for breakfast it was good, but you could always cook." he said licking his lips.

"I'll see you later and we'll find some time to sit down and talk. Bill is just . . . . yeah oh never mind, I'll see you at the wedding." Tiffany said as she turned and walked down the hall to her room to get ready.

Jordan could not help but stand and watch as she moved so perfectly down the hall to her room. "Hmmm . . . . You look too damn good, and you know it to." he whispered and headed out the door.

Putting on the finishing touches she heard the door bell ring. Brushing her hair back behind her ear she went to answer the door. "Hello Bill, come in, I'm just about ready. You can have a seat in the living room." She said pointing to the sofa. "I'll be right back."

"Damn girl, you look amazing. Purple is your color and the way that dress fits you leaves a brotha breathless. I'll wait as long as it takes just to be at your side tonight. You should dress like that for the office." He said with his hand pulling on his goat tee.

"Yes and the other senior partners would really try and get me out of there. Anyway I'm ready; I just had to put my earrings in. So what are we going to do after the reception?"

"I was thinking that we could go to this new little night club. You know do a little dancing, and who knows where the night might end; the day is just getting started. Let's get out of here so we won't be late, and so I can show off my wedding date."

"We are here with ten minutes to spare. Let's sit near the back so if things aren't right we can make an easy exit." Tiffany said walking into the church "Wow everything looks so beautiful they did such a wonderful job on everything." They sat down near the back and in walked Jordan in a black tailored suit looking like he just stepped out of a GQ magazine, and wouldn't you know it, not alone of course. I wonder where he found her. She does not even look old enough to drink, she's cute but that dress she has on is shameful; she is showing almost everything that God gave her and all she added was a little too tight cloth to cover the highlights and hooker heels, he should be ashamed of himself. "Surprise, surprise some things never change." She thought to herself.

Jordan seen Tiffany and turned and sat in the seat right behind her. She could feel her heart starting to race. She turned to talk to Bill, just so she could get a better look at Jordan and his jail bate date. The wedding started, Brenda came down the isle looking like a queen walking down over the freshly fallen red rose petals to meet her king. It was just like a fairy tail come true. After the ceremony Bill rushed her out the door like he did not want anyone to even talk to Tiffany, which was okay because she really was not ready for all of the "Hey girl and how are you doings." She knew the questions and comments would start as soon as people figured out, it was really her. "Slow down Bill, we can't beat the wedding party to their own reception. Can we stop somewhere and have a drink, so I can calm my nerves a bit. That just brought back a lot of old memories and feelings being in that place with all those familiar faces."

"Okay Baby we can go to this little club just down the street; the drinks are cheap but powerful or so I've heard. We don't even have to go to the reception if you are not up to it. We can go to my house and watch a movie and just relax till the clubs start jumping, if you want?"

"No I'll be fine, I just need a quick drink to calm down and so that we won't be the first people at the reception." They arrived at the reception about an hour later. They sat at a table near the door. She felt as if all eyes were on her and Bill who made her feel very uncomfortable but she dealt with it. "Hey girl I heard you were back in town." "It's good to see you out." "Sorry for your loss. Is there anything you need?" "You really haven't gone anywhere since you moved back, have you? Do you want to dance? Let's get you away from people coming up to you for a minute." Bill said taking Tiffany by the hand.

The song seemed to last forever, but Bill was right, it was a breath of fresh air. The DJ turned the music to a slower song and Bill scooped her up in his arms and began singing the words in her ear. "God will this day ever end?" She thought to herself. All during the song she kept on moving his hands back to her waist and away from her butt. One song just seemed to drift right into the next and his grinding seemed to be getting more and more intense. "Hey why don't we seat down for a while." She pulled away from his embrace. "Are you hungry, they have plenty of food over there? Why don't we just go and see what they have." They walked over to the table and as she was about to pick up a napkin from the table, Jordan caught her eye. He was standing off to the side just smiling and observing all of Tiffany's uneasiness. To tired to gather herself together especially now with the extra set of eyes watching her, but it was to no avail as her tension and uneasiness grew more intense with every second she spent with Bill. He was not the man for her, not at all. After all, who comes to a wedding dressed in club clothes? Wow, I must really be going out of my mind.

Bill came up and stood beside her. "Hey Baby you ready to get out of here? This food don't even look good. We can grab a burger or something down the street, so what do you say we do that? You know this wedding getting married stuff is just not for me." He leans in for a kiss. "But I can make it feel like the honeymoon every night."

She puts her hand up to block his kiss, "Hey, you know maybe this wasn't such a good idea. Maybe you should just take me home. I'm kind of tired anyway."

"What are you saying because I said I don't want to get married, the whole evening is over? Ain't this about a bitch! Yeah you are tired alright. Find your own damn way home." As he began to get louder," Are you sure your husband died or did he just leave you. Oh well, I guess he is better off either way."

Jordan walks over "Hey man, I think you need to leave. The lady has a way home, you can leave man!"

"Hey Tiff, are you okay? Come over here and have a seat. Can I get you something to eat or drink whatever you want?" He said offering her a seat at one of the tables.

"Who was that guy? You say you work with him? Enough of the fifty questions just sit here and I'll go get you something to drink."

Jordan returned to the table with two drinks in his hand and handed one to Tiffany. "Thank you Jordan, I really appreciate all of this. I knew that he was a little younger than me, but at work he always seemed so together. Not a street thug made up to look like business man. What am I doing, aren't you here with someone, I can just call a cab. I'll be fine."

"My date? . . . . Oh Tina . . . she'll be okay with this. She has just been coming to my shop hanging out with my assistant Julie and I was talking about the wedding and she had an invitation too so we decided to just go together. So don't trip. She is just here for dancing and the food like everybody else here. Yeah, I think she might have a little crush on me, but there is nothing. Honestly nothing between us." as he turned and pulled a chair up next to Tiffany and sat down.

"I can't go down this road again. We had a past and there is no future." She thought to herself.

"I hope you like this? It was all they had ready and sitting out. I can go back and get you something else, if you don't like this? I can get you something stronger if you want?"

"No this is good, thanks." She said taking another drink from the glass. They sat and talked for what seemed like hours forgetting everyone else there.

Could You Be the One for Me by Brian McKnight started playing, "Can I have this dance?" Hoping that a slow song would calm her down and maybe then they could find sometime for a real discussion. Jordan took her by the hand and led her to the dance floor before she could even get the "yes" all of the way out of her mouth.

All she could think about was him holding her close and how good he looked and smelled. Their bodies just seemed to flow together. It also brought back intimate memories from when they were high school sweethearts.

"Hey baby, who is this? You want to dance when you're done with her?" Tina came up and wrapped her hands around Jordan's arm.

"This is my son Kendall's mother Tiffany and I'm not ready to dance with you right now, maybe in a few songs. When we leave, we are going to give Tiff a ride home. Is that okay with you?"

"If she needs a ride then we need to give her one then, I guess." Tina, looking Tiffany up and down then kind of turning her lip up with disapproval, like who the hell does she thinks she is? "I'll be back, if that's okay with you?"

"I'm sorry Jordan; I can call a cab and go home. It's no big deal. I just can't believe this night; I just want to get out of here. Bill was such a jerk. I'm just going to call a cab and go."

Jordan sat down in the chair next to her, "I'm taking you and that is that." taking his hand and lifting up her head until they were looking into each others eyes. "You hear me?"

"I just don't want to come between you and your date. That's not right and she's obviously upset. You need to go talk to her, and if she says no about the ride home then that is the end of it. I'll catch a cab and it'll be okay. Then you can take your date home and make her a very happy woman tonight."

Jordan got up and turned toward Tiffany, "She's not my date.", and walked up to Tina who had already seemed to have found herself another ride home. Jordan took her aside and started talking to her and she threw up her hands and walked off with some other guy.

Jordan started walking back toward Tiffany. She looked around to avoid looking at him as the lights seemed to dim as he came closer like a tall dark stranger that you just had to turn and take a second look at. Thinking to herself, "I should have just called a cab and went home."

"Can I have this dance?", as he held out his hand to her.

She could not think of or even say the words stop and no, she just followed him onto the dance floor. Following that fragrance, it is so manly and strong, making her want to just melt right there in his arms. "You smell good Jordan; I really like that scent you're wearing. No this can't be right, Jordan, I don't know if it is the wine or what, but I think I need to sit this one out, before I find myself in the corner sick to my stomach or pasted out. Plus I feel as if everyone is just staring at me, at us." She said pulling away.

"It's alright; let me take you home, so you can rest. Wait here and I will pull the car up front, so you don't have to walk too far. Forget what people may be saying or thinking. You wait right here, and I'll be back" He went outside and pulled back up in his black Lincoln Navigator, and politely took her home. "Probably just lying down will make you feel better. Give me a call tomorrow and let me know how you are feeling. Like I told you earlier, you should call in on Monday and take the day off and give that young man a day to really cool down. Cause I don't want to have to show him that I maybe down, but I'm not out. I could bring you by some soup for lunch tomorrow if you would like? I made it yesterday, beef and vegetable. Just let me know." He pulled up in front of her house and walked her to the door. "Now you will be safe from here or do I need to go in and check the place just to make sure."

"Jordan, thank you. You have helped me out enough tonight. I think you are right I am going to take off Monday, the kids will be at school and I can just relax maybe a long soak in the hot tub. I will call you and maybe take you up on your lunch offer. Good night Jordan and thank you again for being my hero. I am sorry about Tina, maybe you should call her" as she got her keys out of her purse and went in the door. She thought Jordan you look to good, not to be attached to someone, and I am not going to play games we are both to old for that.

Chapter 10

● ● ● ● ● ● ● ● ● ● ● ● ● ● ● ● ● ●

"**M**y Christmas this year is really going to be a real let down, the kids are going out of town to Memphis with my dad, because my Grandma called and said that she has not been feeling well. So he and Michelle are going to take the kids with them so they will have something to do over Christmas break beside sit in the house and argue with one another and call me at work every ten minutes to tell me their side of the story before I get home. Dad knew that I couldn't get off work. I know that my time carried over at my job from Virginia to here, but so many other people had already scheduled their time off for vacation before I even came. So I'm, not going to come in rocking the boat. It's not easy as it is, being only one of seven women in an office filled with almost forty men. Jordan I'm sorry I'm just going on and on, you said that you wanted to take some time out to talk. What is it that you want to talk about? Please don't say Kendall. Oh I'm sorry I did not say hi hello or anything I just heard you pick up the phone and I just started talking. Hello Jordan."

"Hello Tiff, and well since you are going to be all alone for Christmas, let's make it fun? My brother Michael and his wife Susan are having a little ice skating party Friday night. They told me that their pond is frozen over and hard enough to skate on. Their going to have some drinks, food, music, games and skating for those of us who dare to take on the pond. Would you like to go? It will be fun, and it will get you out of the house and around adults and not just the people you work with. We will have plenty of time to talk from now until Friday just not over the phone. Relax, don't think of this as a date, just adults hanging out and having fun."

"Adults have fun?" Tiffany said sarcastically. "That does sound like fun. Okay count me in and remember this is not a date, just friends having fun."

"Then let's make it happen."

"Well everyone is leaving this afternoon about one, probably right after Church. They have already packed and are wired for sound. The roads don't look too bad. I don't think that it's going to get bad until later this week, then snow. I think they said about a foot. Now that should be fun to skate in. It has been so long since I went skating. The more I think about it, it really sounds like fun. Count me in. Let me get off this phone so that I can get these kids up and ready for church so we won't be late. Will I see you there?"

"I'll be there, see you then, bye."

* * *

"It's good to see you Tiffany. Where have you been hiding yourself" Rev. Nelson asked

"Just trying to get myself back in the swing of things? I'm doing it slowly but surely. It's getting better and better everyday. Thanks for asking. I enjoyed your sermon today, I will definitely be back to hear more."

"Come on let's get you guys home so you can get on the road, while the roads still look good and safe."

"Do you all have your suitcases in the car? Granddad is ready to go, so let's not keep him waiting. I love you guys and be sure and listen to your granddad and Michelle and your great grandma to; she's not feeling well so be good little helpers. Love you, and don't forget to call me."

Tiffany went in the house and made a grilled cheese sandwich and some tomato soup. The door bell rang, "Who could be ringing the door bell now, I just got in the house?" She thought to herself.

She opened the door it was Jordan. "Jordan I thought we would be meeting a little later. Come on in, would you like something to eat?"

"Sure I forgot how you loved to cook and eat, but never seemed to gain any weight by doing it and never exercised. You know how many women must hate you for that? Sure I'll have whatever you're having. Kendall said you really did up the place. He told me that in the spring you were going to do some landscaping? You know I know someone that could really cut you a deal and do a really good job. Let me get you his card." Jordan said as he pulled one of his business cards out of his wallet.

"Why thank you. I will have to give him a call in the spring when I am ready to get something done out here. So I have heard you do a real good job at this landscaping stuff. How long have you been doing it for?"

"I have had my store for about eight years, but I have been really getting some real return customers for about six. I do some of the older people in the Church yards for free. I told Kendall that he could help me out this year if he wanted to earn a little spending money and learn a little to. He told me that he would like to learn. He said that he wants to own his own business when he gets older. Not to change the subject, but how have you been. I mean after the death of David and then moving back here and leaving everything behind. I'm sure that was not easy?"

"I'm adjusting and taking it one day at a time, but being back home with my family is good for me, and I was able to transfer with my job. So I didn't loose anytime or benefits so that is another good thing. I guess all and all I am doing well."

Jordan stood up and leaned over to kiss her on the forehead. "You look a little tired. I will call you later and tell you more about Friday. Thanks for the food, I really needed it, it was really good." Jordan said as he put his coat on and pulled some lip balm out of his pocket to slide over his already very soft lips. He turned and said, "Until Friday then."

* * *

The week went by slowly, and Jordan's lips kept running through Tiffany's mind, as she laid there in bed. Then the phone started ringing bringing her back down to earth.

"Good morning Tiffany, thought I'd give you a wake up call to get you up and going. I wanted to call you and remind you about tonight and that I should be by to get you about six, don't forget to pack a change of clothes just incase yours gets wet or something, you'll have something to put on. Last but not least, have a great day at work today, and don't work too hard. You'll need your energy for tonight."

"Good morning Jordan. I already have everything ready for tonight. It sounds like it is going to be so much fun, I can't wait. I am only working a half-a-day today, because we are closing out a lot of accounts for the holiday and opening them back up for the New Year. So today should be pretty easy for me. See you about six then. Good bye."

After hanging up the phone from him she felt all warm inside, a feeling that she had not felt since David and never thought she would feel again especially not with Jordan. Maybe he has changed, only time will tell. Dad and Kendall can't both be wrong. Can they? We just have to really talk all playing aside. There are so many things that need to be said and talked about. I can't just chalk it up to that was in the past and we were young but it's okay now that we have grown up.

Where are those skates, I thought I sat them right down here by the door so I would not forget them. Figures I put them back in the closet, she thought to herself. She could see Jordan truck pulling up in the driveway.

There goes the doorbell. Tiffany opened the door, "Hello! Are you about ready?"

"Yes, I just need to pick up my bag and purse and we are on our way."

"You sure you got enough on? It's cold out here tonight and we are going to be right on the pond and outside?"

"I have on layers from long underwear to t-shirts to sweaters, jeans, socks, a coat, gloves, a hat, and boots. Oh, I will be warm! What about you? Doesn't look like you could fit too much more in those jeans" she said with a bit of a flirty smile.

He turned and looked at her and just bit his bottom lip, "Oh wow." He opened the truck door.

"Okay we will see how all of that holds up against the elements. Let me get your bag, Michael and Susan are waiting for us. Her parents have their kids this weekend so they are letting their hair down and playing like kids. Michael and I went hunting a while back, and the deer sausage is from us and our hunting. They have a new house just on the outskirts of town. So they call it generic country living. They like it, so it's good. The kids love it so they can have all of the animals that they want, as long as they clean up after them that is. You remember Susan, don't you? She started going to school with us the end of our senior year, she was a junior. She never hung out and did all that crazy stuff like some those girls did. Once Michael seen her he was hooked. They got married after college and started having kids soon after. They have three, my niece Alisha and my two nephews Terry and Gregory, love then to death, they are rotten. That's enough talk let's get down this road." Jordan said turning the truck down the street to drive.

"I don't remember Susan, but if she stole Michael's heart and they are making babies then she must be pretty special. I remember back in school he was a real ladies man and was not even thinking about settling down with anyone for even nine months to have a kid, never the less be a family man? Wow, that's real nice. I can't wait to meet her."

Now that we have some time, let's talk. I heard you and Brooklyn got married and then everyone said it was like she just disappeared off the face of the earth. What was the deal with that?"

"Well when the NBA scouts were looking at me; she was all over me, you know my biggest cheerleader. We got married, then a couple of bad playing years in college, and all those positive pregnancy tests kept on being wrong. The trips to Europe kept getting longer and longer until I finally got divorce-papers in the mail and it was over. Now she is married to a man that cheats on her left and right; they have two kids together and she's unhappy. She called me about five years ago and was telling me how she wanted to come back home, and how she was over being over seas. I told her that there was no hope for us ever again. Then a few weeks after that, she sent me a bunch of pictures of her naked and in a lot of different poses telling me that we could try some of them when she got back home. That's the last I heard from her. A road too many have traveled on, is not the road I'm going down anymore."

"So Kendall is your only child?"

"My only son, not to say if the right woman came along, I would start right away making more, I love kids Tiffany, always have always will. When you left Tiff, you never even turned around to ask, to check, nothing. Went off had Kendall and next thing I knew your dad was announcing in Church that you had gotten married. That was all that Brooklyn wanted to hear. She was out the next week picking out wedding rings. She never stopped to think that I could have been hurting and wanting and needing answers. She was there and I thought that I loved her and she told me she was pregnant. So I did the right thing this time I thought so, I married her. My game was just completely off, the agents started not to show too much interest anymore then surprise, surprise she was not pregnant anymore. She said that the test must have been wrong, I guess the doctors to. My game started picking up and look who's pregnant again, only to lose it when the agents stopped looking again. Come on this is going to be a good evening full of family, friends and fun, not bad decisions of the past. Just over the hill and we are there at Michael and Susan's, to begin our night of fun."

"Smile Jordan, the night is ours and we are going to laugh and have fun!" Tiffany said leaning over and squeezing his leg.

* * *

"Hey Michael, where should we put our stuff?"

"Over in the guest room Jordan. Quit acting like a stranger man. Who is this beautiful lady you have with you brother dear? Tiffany, Tiffany, Tiffany you are a sight for soar eyes. Long time no see, and you have not changed a bit. Jordan you better not let this one get away again."

"Thank you Michael and you must be Susan? Jordan told me a lot about you on our drive up. I can't say I remember from school. Well anyway it's good to meet you and from what Jordan says, it's going to be fun. So here I am let's get this party started."

"Tiffany, if you want, we can get started with skating and have them join us after they get everything put away and get some more logs on the fire outside. There are no kids here this weekend and I am going to enjoy myself. This house is never this peaceful; I can't believe it."

"Okay if that's the case let's get on our skates and go." As Tiffany moved outside with Susan, all she could think about was Jordan and the conversation on the ride, you are here for fun not a get some getaway? Please.

"Come on there are already a few couples outside. We are expecting about six or eight more people, if it gets too cold, we can just come in and play board games or watch some movies."

Jordan came out and sat down on a log next to Tiffany and put his skates on. "Jordan it has been years since I did this, so you are going to have to hold me until I get sure of myself and balanced. Okay?"

"Come on Tiff, let yourself go, it's easy baby come on." Jordan said pulling her up and onto the ice. "What you thought I would complain about you asking me to hold you?"

"Damn it!" Tiffany fell down to the ground.

"Are you okay? Here let me help you up." He said chuckling

"Give me a second and I will have this down." She said laughing.

"They are playing a slow song can we skate together under the stars and the moon together?"

"Why yes. Yes we can." Smiling and taking Jordan by the hand and not noticing a large rock sticking out from the ice. They made it through almost the whole song, when all of the sudden Tiffany spun out of control ending up at the base of an old oak tree.

"Baby are you okay? Be still. You are going to have to calm down so we can see what has happened."

"My leg, I think it's broken! It hurts!" Tiffany cried out doubling up in pain.

"Jordan man, pick her up and get her in the house and onto the couch or on one of the beds." Michael ordered.

"I'm just going to slide your skate off. I know that it is going to hurt, but we need to get it off. We can cut it off if that will be better for you?"

"Tiff, listen to Susan, she's an RN so she knows what she is talking about. Do you want us to cut the skate off you? We can?" Jordan said holding onto Tiffany's hand as if would take the pain away by doing so.

"Cut it off, god please cut it off!" She shouted gasping for breath. "Oh this hurts so bad, is it broken? Oh this hurts."

"Your foot and ankle look pretty swollen and I do see some bleeding. We can either take you in one of the trucks to the hospital or call an ambulance and go. Either way you need to get to a hospital and quickly."

After that was said Tiffany looked down at her foot and fainted. She woke up a little later in the hospital. Jordan felt that he could out drive any ambulance to get Tiffany to the hospital.

"Hey are you okay?" The doctor said that you are probably going to have to stay off your feet for a couple of weeks. It looks like when you fell a branch got into your skate and when you hit the base of that tree, the branch is what hit first and it went right into the side of your ankle and scratched you up pretty bad and caused a lot of swelling but you should be back on your feet in no time. He gave you a prescription for pain; we can get it filled on our way to your house. If you like, I'm sure you will need some more before the morning."

"Thank you so much for being there for me. I think that we better stop and get that filled. I don't want to wake up crying out in pain. I'm laughing but it hurts already. Can they give me something before we get out of here?"

"I'll tell the doctor that he needs to put some more of that good stuff in your IV before we get out of here and get you tucked in bed and comfortable." kissing her once again.

They stopped by the pharmacy on the way to Tiffany's house, "Give me your keys. Let me get out and unlock your door. Now this is my chance to carry you over the threshold. I do. I will, now and forever more. You just have that affect on a man begging for a second chance at happiness. You think you could give me that chance?" He looked down at her to see that she had fallen fast asleep in his arms. He took her in the house and laid her down across the bed and placed a blanket over her and took the shoe off her other foot, then kissed her on the lips. "Good night my love, I'll be over here if you need me for anything."

He pulled up a chair and stool up to rest my legs on next to her bed and threw a blanket over himself to keep warm. "Could there really be a chance for me, for us after all of this time" He whispered in the air as he turned and looked at her sleeping so sweetly.

His pocket began to vibrate with an incoming call, "Who is calling me so late? Private calls, I don't do." Jordan looks at his phone and pressed the ignore button. "Wow two private calls and the last one even left a message." he says and sat his cell phone down on her nightstand next to her bed. "There will be no secrets between us ever again." He turns the lights out and pulls a blanket up.

"Good morning Jordan, how did I get here? What are you doing here? Oh ouch . . . I remember now my ankle is killing me. Did we pick up my prescription? I think I am going to need it right away, if you don't mind?" looking as if she had swallowed the worst tasting pill of her life.

"Good morning, it's almost noon." he chuckled "I got your medicine last night on the way to your house. I thought I would hang around in case you needed me for anything when you woke up, I would be right here and ready. I hope you don't mind, I was looking around in your refrigerator and thought I would cook you up a little something. So sit up, sit back, and relax, and enjoy. I'm here to serve you and only you, so your request is my command. You know kind of like your wish is my command thing. I'll give you some medicine once you have eaten a little something."

After they ate a little breakfast Jordan stood up, "I am going to wash these few dishes up and head down to the store for a couple hours, so if you need me call and you get some rest."

"I'll see you later, and I will call if I need you." looking as if there was something else she really wanted to say.

Just then his phone rang "Your phone is ringing. Do you want me to get it?"

"Sure answer it if you want."

"Hello" "Hello" Tiffany repeated. "Guess they did not want to talk to me. Here you go, here's your phone. Just in case I need to call you. Why don't you take my keys, so when you come back, I won't have to try and limp to the door and be in pain"

"Thanks see you in a little bit." Jordan leans over and kisses her on the lips. "Nice."

Chapter 11

● ● ● ● ● ● ● ● ● ● ● ● ● ● ● ● ● ● ● ●

J ordan's phone started vibrating in his pocket when he got into his truck. He looked down at the caller ID, "Damn another private call." He answered it, "Hello? What do you mean? How's it going? You can't just pop in and out of someone's life whenever the time is right for you. Brooklyn what do you mean we are still married and our daughter is now ten years old. Have you lost your freakin' mind? You can't do this to me all over again . . . and over the phone? Tiffany is never going to believe this. I can't do this to her again, she deserves better than this. What do you mean you're in town and we need to talk? You are not going to do this to me again. I won't let you, not again. Okay let's get this over with, where do you want to meet?"

"Okay I'll be there in an hour, and don't you dare be late!"

* * *

"Brooklyn" Jordan said with an over load of baritone in his voice.

"Jordan" Brooklyn replied rolling her eyes and snarling her nose at him.

"What brings you back to town after all these years and what do you mean we are still married? This can't be right I signed all of the papers and everything you sent me. I even kept a copy for myself, so no bullshit like this would ever happen, and look what happens. You said I have a daughter? Where is she? What's her name? How could you have kept something like this hidden from me? You don't have the right. You can't just play with peoples lives, people aren't games. Taking them out and putting them up when you are ready, and to hell with everyone else. Brooklyn, I want some answers."

"Jordan all we have to do is go in front of a judge and he can sign the papers. I was just to busy too stop and get it done. Your daughter Trina, like I said she is ten. You can have all of the blood test you want she's yours. I just thought that it was time the two of you meet. Oh and look who is back in your little life again, Tiffany. What will she think and what will she do? Poor little Tiffany is going to just come unglued. Get over it. Pay me child support and she never even has to know. We will be your dirty little secret back in New York, and you can have the real love of your life."

"You have really lost it. Are you following me now? You can just keep Tiffany out of this; she and I have suffered enough because of you . . . because of us. I will get an attorney and we will handle this in the courts, and Tiffany will know all. This meeting is over. See you in court that is if what you are telling me is the truth."

"Oh it's true. I will see you there."

"You told me that you lost the baby? You know we are getting paternity test don't you? You fooled me before with your confessions of love and how much you wanted to be with me and have a family, but then all of the men, the trips, the late hours, the all niters, and the phone calls. You were better than those nine hundred numbers with all of the service you were providing to all of your men friends. You went out of town, came back and said you and your friends were playing around on the bleachers and fell and lost the baby, then you said you had to leave and be alone for awhile. Then the next thing I knew, I was getting divorce papers in the mail. Come on you know I signed them! The last thing I wanted was to be married to someone who didn't want to be married to me, and wanted to be with everyone else. No thanks! Why are you doing this? Why now? What all of your men friends are seeing you for what you really are? A gold digging . . . ."

"Jordan shut up already! I see how you feel. Let's just hope your little Tiffany feels the same! I am sure it will seem, like high school all over again, but she's not pregnant again, is she? That would be a real shame. Still married to the big bad Brooklyn, and screwing little miss perfect, and what another little high school backyard incident thing poor little Tiffany. Well anyway, see yeah in court. Hope you have a good attorney." Brooklyn said as she jumped in her car and sped off in a huff.

Jordan stood cold, still and steaming. "I can't do this to Tiffany again; she has been hurt by me enough. I can't put her through this, but I love her. I love her so damn much. I can't lose her not again over someone so stupid." slamming the door so hard that the glass shattered on impact. "My day has to get better!"

His cell phone began to ring. "Hello Julie. What can I do for you?"

"Well, Mrs. Greentree called and wants to know if you could come by and put some salt out in her driveway and on porch and sidewalk. She's afraid that she is going to hurt herself if she falls on it. You know she thinks you are handsome and she just wants you over there to look at. By the way how's Ms. Tiffany doing this morning, I heard that her ankle was pretty banged up. I hope she's okay, but I'm sure she will be just fine with a big strong man there looking after her every want and need." Julie said giggling.

"Julie I'm going to swing by the office and pick up one of the work trucks. The glass broke in the window of my truck. And yes Miss Thang, Tiffany is at home resting; I'll be going by and check on her a little later. Do we have any other calls pending after I get done with Mrs. Greentree? You are just mad that she can call me, and I'll come and clear her path to me any day of the week and all she has to do is smile." Jordan said smiling.

"Okay I will pull one outside and warming up for you when you get here. No, that's all the calls in for today"

"Thanks Julie, if you just leave it locked up in the fence. I won't be out that long and you can go ahead and take off. If you look in my desk drawer there's an envelope in there for you. Have a good Christmas and I'll see you after your vacation."

Julie was Jordan office assistant she did everything in the office filing, appointments, making and taking calls, making fliers, typing letters and ordering supplies, it was her all her and she had been doing it now for over six years, and she was the best. He hoped that she would take the three hundred dollar Christmas bonus he left her in an envelope in his desk drawer and not try and give it back, but that was the way Julie was. She was married and they had one little girl that she could spend it on and enjoy.

"Damn it a little girl with that demon bitch Brooklyn. How could this be happening? I need to tell Tiff everything, I don't I need to wait until I can give her all of the answers she's going to want to know, I just need to tell her everything that I know now. God let me know the right thing to do before I go and hurt Tiff all over again. Give me a clue, just a little one, please."

*   *   *

"Hey Tiff, how's the ankle? Have you been keeping it elevated? What can I fix you to eat?" Jordan said going into the bedroom of Tiffany's house after he let himself in using her keys she had given him that morning.

"I have been a good girl; I have kept my leg up and only went to the restroom once since you've been gone. I don't know what I am going to do about work on Tuesday, since Monday we are off for Christmas. The kids are coming home early, because I called and told them what happened and Dad said that he was going to be leaving out on Wednesday so they can spend some time taking care of me." She was hoping that he would jump in and come up with some excuse for the kids to stay longer so they could have a little more alone time together, but to her shock nothing. In fact a kind of cold reaction to everything she had said. It was like he was a million miles away, on his own planet. Maybe it's just me. "Jordan, are you hungry? I can order in some Chinese, if you like?" She looked at him and he was off on some distant planet. "Hello! Are you in there somewhere Jordan? What's wrong with you?"

"I'm sorry Tiff. I just found out about a new project that I really need to start working on. I don't know how these things just come up from out of nowhere and just wreck havoc on everything around. It just pisses me off. I'm not ready for this one at all. You know on top of everything, I broke the window out in my truck, that's why I'm in the work truck." He stopped when he noticed the confused look on Tiffany's face. "I'm sorry Tiff; you said something about getting something to eat? Whatever you want to get is fine with me. Like I told you before I am all yours, your every wish is my command."

"I was just going to order some Chinese. I wanted to thank you for taking care of me last night and staying here, you know you really didn't have to and also picking up our order of Chinese food when it's ready, please." Tiffany said shyly.

"I can stay again, if you like? No funny stuff. I will even sleep on the couch or in the other bedroom if you want me to?"

"You really don't have to. Let's just get through dinner and we'll see what happens next."

Jordan came back with dinner; they ate along with very little small talk.

"Are you done? You know you have to open your fortune cookie and read it." Tiffany said handing him one of the cookies.

"Okay here goes." he said smiling "You will meet a difficult challenge with a smile. Let's hope that's true because I have a difficult one in front of me."

"Okay, okay here's mine. You are at the start of a new beginning take it slow, but be open."

"If you move much slower, we'll both be asleep." he said taking the chance to lean in and kiss her. Tiffany was enjoying the kiss when his phone started ringing.

"Hello? . . . . You need to stop calling me! I said that I would have my attorney to contact you, about you and your child; therefore we have nothing else to talk about until there is a court date set. Good bye!"

"Is everything okay?" Tiffany said with a confused look on her face.

Jordan looked at Tiffany then shook his head and looked back into her eyes, "No Tiffany, its Brooklyn. She started calling me last night telling me that we're still married and that I have a ten year old daughter. I signed all the papers years ago, and sent them back to her. A daughter . . . . she has got to be lying again, back to all of her old tricks. You know, I hate to cut this evening short, but maybe we should. I have something I need to get started working on. I want to make sure what we're doing or maybe doing is right. Like I told you, I really need to get to the bottom of this whole thing. I think I need to leave, are you going to be able to get around and get everything you need on your own tonight?"

Tiffany just sat still on the sofa for a minute letting things just stink in, "I can't believe this. You and Brooklyn doing this to me all over again, at least this time I'm not pregnant or falling for your bullshit lies. I think you need to leave and make sure you leave my keys at the door on your way out. I'm sure you are needed at home with your family or something. You won't be living two lives on my account! Get out Jordan!" Tiffany screamed as tears ran down her face.

"You don't understand. I don't even understand everything myself this time. I just need time to do this." He went to reach for her.

"No! . . . . Jordan it is time for you to leave, and don't forget my key! No! You are not going to do this to me again. That's what I get for listening to people telling me how you've changed! Get out!" Tiffany yelled at Jordan as she clutched onto one of the decorative pillows on her sofa.

"I'm sorry Tiffany; I would never want to hurt you again. You have to believe me when I tell you that. All I can tell you now is that I'm sorry."

With hurt and anger in her voice all could say was, "For the last time Jordan, get out! I'm done!" Jordan walked out the door with a bowed head and pained look on his face, and placed her keys on the holder by the door, locked the bottom lock on the door and left.

*   *   *

Two weeks later after calling and leaving phone message after phone message for Tiffany. "Damn now this court papers mailed to my business address. Brooklyn suing me for a divorce and child support. This is a hell of a way to start my morning, and my new year, suit papers. Julie, get my attorney on the phone and let him know that they've arrived. Tell him that we need to meet today, because I want this done and over with quickly. I'll be in my office when you get that done"

Julie got on her phone right away and started dialing, "Jordan, I have your attorney on the phone and Kendall here to see you."

"Julie I'll take the call and tell Kendall I will come get him as soon as I'm off of the phone."

After a little less than an hour of talking with his attorney Jordan hung up the phone, and walked out of his office to get his son. "Kendall, come on in son. What brings you down here?"

"Mom told me that you have another family, is that true dad? Where do they live and why have you been keeping them a secret from me?"

"Those are all good questions son, but I don't have an answer for you because I don't know the answers myself. One thing I can tell you son, is that I was never told anything about them." He went on to tell Kendall a little bit about what was going on with Brooklyn and her news of a child and not being divorced, but ask that he didn't say anything to Tiffany because he wanted to have all the answers for her when the time came to talk to her, and he didn't want for her to be hurt anymore especially not by him again because he loved her and wanted a second chance, free from stress and problems. He also told Kendall not to tell his mom that he had come by the store to talk and find out what was going on.

"Dad let me get out of here because mom will be calling around looking for me. I hope everything you're telling is true and I hope that everything works out right for you dad. Mom needs someone good in her life, and I think that could be you. I just hope it works out this time. You know mom's birthday is coming up and that would be a great gift for her just to hear good news. Things are going to work dad." Kendall said leaving out the door.

"I hope you are right son, because I need your mother in my life to." He picks up the court papers and starts looking over them again.

Chapter 12

● ● ● ● ● ● ● ● ● ● ● ● ● ● ● ● ● ● ●

The day before they were to go to court Jordan's attorney called him. "Jordan I got a call from Brooklyn's attorney and they want to settle out of court. She said that the papers that you signed ten years ago were legal and they're just going to present them in front of a judge here in town and everything will be in effect as of the date that you signed them. As far as the child, you don't need to worry about that either, she was trying to scam you out of money. There was already a child support hearing held in which they found out who the father was and that he was paying child support until he died last year and then the family gave her an additional fifty thousand dollars in death benefits from a life insurance policy, that they didn't even have to. Just guess the man's wife felt that it was only right to give the child something, so she gave her the money for the child support to be held in a trust fund when she turns eighteen not to Brooklyn. That is one hell of a woman; I know my wife would have said to hell with her and her baby and that all that money was hers and our kids. So no court date for you for tomorrow or ever, concerning Brooklyn, it's over."

"Dan, you just don't know how good you have made this day become, so no court tomorrow right? I don't even need to be there when the judge signs off on those papers? All right then. I have some things I need to do today. Yes! It's a great day." He hung up the phone from his attorney and dialed Tiffany's work number, "Yes I would like to know if Tiffany Morgan is in the office today? Well I just need to know what the address is to the office . . . . Okay thank you very much."

He hung up the phone and dialed the number of a near by floral shop. "Yes I would like to have two dozen red long stem roses delivered to Tiffany Morgan at 828 W High Ave, and on the card I want to it to say "I love you and I'm sorry for everything, can we talk? Love Jordan." and could you make sure that she can have them before four o'clock before she leaves the office today?"

Later that evening the phone rang, Jordan looked at his caller ID, which displayed the name Tiffany Morgan. "Hello."

"Hello, Jordan I got the flowers, they're beautiful. So you're sorry? Are you going to tell me about it, or should I just keep guessing about what is going on with you and your family? By the way, thank you for the flowers." She added sarcastically.

"Tiffany, can we talk over dinner tonight? By the way how's your ankle doing? Are you able to get around on it pretty good?"

"Dinner, what time? Are you going to come by here and pick me up or do you just want to meet somewhere?" Hoping that he would just say that he would bring something over and they could eat in front of the fire place because she would feel more secure on her own turf. Plus she didn't really want to get out with her ankle in this weather. She had a feeling that whatever he had to say this time had to be good, especially with the flowers and the card saying he was sorry and that he loved her, and they looked beautiful in the center of the dinning room table card included.

"I will be by in about an hour to get you." Jordan hung up the phone. "Now is my chance to explain everything to her and make her understand that I was not trying to keep anything from her and that everything I had told her before was true and that the only thing I wanted to do was to win her heart back. She's everything that a woman should be and if I could, I want to spend the rest of my life showing her that she is that woman and that I'm every bit of the man that she needs." He said aloud

One hour later he was there ringing her doorbell, Tiffany opened the door. "Hey you look beautiful tonight. Are you ready? You know we are supposed to get a real bad snow storm coming through tonight? Are you sure you are dressed warm enough? I'm not complaining because that skirt and sweater look great on you. Is that Ace bandage around your ankle going to be enough with those heels lookin all sexy?" He said looking her down from head to toe.

"We're not going skating again, or eating around a camp fire are we?" Tiffany said laughing. "I'll be fine just let me grab my coat."

"This evening we're just going to go back to my place. I cooked a roast and the perfect pineapple upside down cake for desert and the fireplace is going. I think we need to relax and have a private talk. Does that sound okay to you?"

"I'll let you lead the way. I'm in your hands tonight. Keep me warm and safe and you're good." She said rather flirty.

They got to Jordan's house, he pulled in the driveway, he got out opened her door and led her to the front door and opened it. Inside the lights were dimmed in the living room by the fire place that seemed to just caress his off white colored leather furniture with a soft glow that made it just look all warm and cozy and in the dinning room the table was set for two with a bouquet of wild flowers in the center and candles surrounding it.

"Would you like to start with eating dinner in here, or have conversation over there?" Jordan said pointing in the direction of the dimly lit living room.

"I think better on a full stomach, and besides that I want to enjoy some of your fine cooking, and easy conversation will come later." She said hanging her coat up on a rack in his foyer.

"You are walking pretty good, can I get you something to drink, a glass of wine, tea or water with your dinner?", as he pulls the chair out for her to sit.

"Wine would be fine and can I have a glass of water with that to please?" Dinner went by without a hitch and they moved into the living room for desert and conversation. He went on to explain everything that had happened with Brooklyn and her daughter. It kind of hit home, when he got to the part about her being paid fifty thousand dollars because the girl's father had died in April, because after David had died, and Tiffany got the money from his life insurance policies. She went to her attorney and talked with a child support attorney on her husband's child support case, and she paid out fifty thousand dollars since the woman never wanted David or me to have anything to do with the child and they lived in New York. So David just paid out the support and agreed never to ask anymore questions about the girl. So when he died, she just thought that it would be right that she should get something, and it would end any further obligation from me or any member of David's family. Tiffany explained all of this to Jordan, they both agreed that it was just too much of a coincidence and that they would both do some more digging into it, because the whole thing just didn't sound right. They laughed and talked more about their lives and some of the things they had gone through. Jordan stopped talking and leaned in and gave her a kiss on the lips.

The tension was so thick in the air between them, but they could both feel the heat rising between them. "Jordan are you sure we are ready for this, and you're sure you have told me everything I need to know. No skeletons lying in the back of your closet, because these are my feelings and they are real and I need to be able to trust you." She said pulling away from more advances.

"I'm not going to rush you and I'm not going to force you to do anything with me. I'm going to tell you that I do know that when I was young I let the best thing that ever came my way go because I was a stupid horny teenager. Now I'm grown and know what I want out of life, and know who I want in my life and that's you. You're right, we are not going to rush this. We're going to take it slow, however long that takes, I'll be here waiting. Don't worry that I'm going to be out with other women, because that's not what I'm about, besides there's no other woman that's going to do. I love you Tiffany." looking her in the eyes.

Tiffany looked away from his stare because she felt so confused. "Not to change the subject, but can we turn on the news to see if all of that snow they were talking about is still on its way? I'm hoping they're wrong, and it's just going to pass over us. Jordan, I felt it to; there is something there between us and not just because of Kendall. There's like a magic or energy when we are together." Tiffany stopped and looked at the TV, "Did you hear that they're saying they don't want anyone out on the roads tonight if you don't have to be? Can I use your phone, my phone is dead. I need to call and check on the kids, they are with my Dad and Michelle tonight. You know Dad steals them every chance he gets, he thinks that he is making up for all of the years he missed when we lived in Norfolk." reaching for the glass of wine sitting on the table she accidentally knocks it over on herself. "Damn it. I can't believe I did this. Do you have something I can use to clean this up? I need to rinse this out before it stains this sweater and skirt."

Just then the lights went out. "Hang on Tiff; let me grab one of the candles in the other room. I'll get them and get you something to put on. Just be still and don't move, I don't want to fall on you. Well at least not like that." he chuckled and went down the hall.

"Funny Jordan, just hurry up."

He came back in the room and took her by the hand and led her down the hall and led through an open door into a guest bedroom. "I have set you up in my guest room, I laid out a t-shirt and some pajama bottoms on the bed, I hope they're not too big for you. There are candles in the bathroom next door, so that you can have light to rinse your clothes out. If you need me I am right down the hall, just yell and I'll be right there." he said licking his lips and looking at her with those tell me what you need and it's yours eyes.

"Thanks Jordan, I think I can handle this." As she went into the guest room, Jordan went to his room and put on some pajamas.

As he was coming back down the hall, he noticed that the door to the guest room was not completely closed. He stopped in the hall and looked in. There stood Tiffany with nothing on but the amber glow of the candles, lighting every inch of her magnificent body. She pulled the t-shirt on over her head and he could not tell that this was the body of a woman that had carried three children; her body still looked as firm and together as it did when they were teenagers. She took care of her body and those nonstop long sexy legs. "I need this woman back in my life, forever this time." He whispered, needing to walk away from this view to help him control stiffing parts on his body.

Tiffany came in the living room twirling around, "So what do you think, how do I look?" She said blinking, winking and flirting.

"Amazing simply amazing." he responded in his deep sexy voice he stopped her from twirling and held her in his arms. "How could I have been such a fool?" then kissed her freshly glossed lips. "Tiffany." He said calling her name as he brushed the hair from in front of her eyes. "I love you; I'm not a little teenage boy with a hard-on. I'm a grown man with his head on right and know what he wants not just a one night stand but for life. I am not going to hurt you, I did that and lost everything that I loved to another man who stepped to the plate and won your heart but I want to tell you now this time is forever." as they started kissing by the light of the fire place.

"Jordan I knew that I still had feelings for you just by the way my dad and Kendall were singing your praises the minute I got back into town, and then on Thanksgiving when you kissed me. I swear I could feel your lips touching mine for weeks after that. I stopped and took a second look at what they were saying, and I agreed there was something different about you, something I wanted to learn more about." Jordan stopped her from talking and the kissing became more passionate as they sat down on the couch and started acting like teenagers in high school in the back seat of a car.

"Let's move into another room." he said standing up and taking her by the hand and leading her down the hall to his bedroom.

Chapter 13

● ● ● ● ● ● ● ● ● ● ● ● ● ● ● ● ● ●

T hey stood at the foot of his bed and he got on his knees. Looking up at her, "Do you need these on?" as he pulled the drawstring to her pajama bottoms. They instantly feel to the floor covering her feet and her body with nothing but the amber glow of candle light and a white lacy pair of panties. He guided her to sit on the edge of the bed, he parted her legs massaging her thighs, laughing softly as he seen her birth mark on the inside of her right thigh. "Still there just like I remembered, I guess this will be my starting point." as he began kissing her right there on her birthmark, while his hands guided her panties down her legs, then he opened up her legs even further, he took his fingers and began rubbing inside and outside of her pleasure point, as she leaned back to allow him greater access to explore, soon his mouth moved into to join in on the pleasure his fingers were supplying to his queen, he began kissing, licking, sucking in a rhythm that sent waves of pleasure through her. She sat up grabbing his head unable to stand it any longer. "Lay back, I want to taste all of the pleasure that I am making you feel." she caught her breath and laid back as he requested and he continued on with his pleasing until at last he knew she was done. He pulled her up removing his t-shirt he had given her to wear and his pajamas that he had put on to make her feel comfortable. There he stood fully erect and shining in the glow. He went over to his night stand and pulled out a condom.

"Here, let me help you with that." taking it out of his hands and opening up the package and taking it out. "It's time for you to sit down now." as she slid the condom on him and climbed on top of him putting him inside of her and began a rhythm that caused Jordan to cry out with moans of delight, taking his finger and massaging her pleasure, sending her in a whirlwind of uncontrolled ecstasy, "Jordan, oh Jordan!"

He sat up still holding her body tightly and keeping rhythm looked in her eyes, "Tiffany you are so sexy." turning her over so that he was on top as she wrapped her legs around him so that he could go deeper, and as he went deeper the moans came out of Tiffany, he leaned in to her ear and started growling like an animal taking over his pray until they both cried out as their bodies could take no more. "I love you Tiffany."

"Oh Jordan, I love you too." as she turned over so that her back was to him, he pulled her wet hot body in close and put his arm around her and they fell breathlessly asleep.

The next morning they woke up to the sound of his phone ringing. "No Julie I'm up. Okay well let me just, say I'm up now." He said yawning and looking over at Tiffany just starting to open her eyes.

"Julie called me, and I need to be out helping clean off the streets from all of this snow we got last night. By the way the power is back on. Will you be alright if I take you home after I get done?" He questioned and got up and layed out some clothes.

"I'll be fine just being a little lazy Jordan, just hanging out waiting on you. Do you want something to eat before you leave for work?'

"No I'll be alright, but please feel free and help yourself to whatever you want, or you can just lay there and look sexy and wait till I get back home." he pulled out the ironing board as he began ironing his jeans for work. He sat at the edge of the bed and put them on and leaned over and kissed her on the neck as she laid there with her back to him watching the television.

That one kiss sent waves of emotions through her more lasting than any night of love making could have ever done. It was from Jordan and it was perfect, so sweet, and so innocent wanting nothing more.

Later that day he drove her home to find that the kids were there safe and sound with her dad and Michelle waiting at the house for her to return. When she came through the door Ken turned around and looked at her with that all knowing fatherly look, "So how has your day been today? Did you help Jordan clear the roads? Did the two of you get a chance to talk, really talk?" He said looking at her over the top of his glasses.

"Dad I think that is enough, I'm a big girl now, and yes Dad we did get a chance to talk and clear the air about a lot of questions the two of us had. You are right; I think he has grown up quite a bit since high school. He is out there now cleaning off the driveway and sidewalk. He went up and down the street a couple of times, so that if I needed to get out and go anywhere I could"

"I'm glad you guys got some of those things worked out. I know it will take some time, but keep talking and listening. It works." Ken said leaving out as he patted Jordan's shoulder as he came in house from the snow and cold.

Jordan came in and sat down at the kitchen table, "Did I miss something?"

"No. It is just dad being dad. So what are you doing for dinner tonight?"

"I was just going to warm up some of the roast from last night, watch a little television and turn in early. You know you wore me out last night and this afternoon?" he said leaning over to kiss her lips." I think the street crews have done a pretty good job in getting everything cleared off and cleaned up. I have a few more things that I have to do before I go home. The kids were outside watching me work. Anyway let me get out of here. I'll call you a little bit later this evening. I love you." with another kiss on her lips before leaving out the door.

"I love you too Jordan, I'll talk to you this evening. If the kids are still outside, tell them to come in, it's getting kind of dark out there."

Jordan got in his truck, "First things first, blow her mind with Valentine's Day then make her mine a few day's later on her birthday." He said looking back in the windows of her house from the driver's seat in his truck.

* * *

"Good morning Charlotte, and Happy Valentine's day. I hope you got what you wanted today. If not I am sure he'll make it up tonight." Charlotte was the office receptionist and had been with the company for over twenty years, and was loved by everyone in the office and at home by her husband of twenty years.

"Good morning Tiffany, I just put something in your office, you might want to see. Happy Valentine's Day to you too, I made some coffee; it's in the break room, if you want some. Don't you look lovely this morning; it must have been a good night?" Charlotte said as she handed Tiffany a stack of files to look over.

"Thanks. I know what I will be doing today." Tiffany said rolling her eyes. "I'll be in my office, if anyone is looking for me." she said heading down the hall and opens her office door. "Oh my God." Her office is filled with red, white and pink balloons and a bouquet of wild flowers in the middle of her desk along with a card, I LOVED YOU ONCE AND I AM GLAD I GOT THE CHANCE TO DO IT AGAIN. LOVE JORDAN.

"What am I going to do with you?" She said the minute Jordan answered his phone.

"So I take it that you're at work? I feel asleep last night and did not get a chance to call you back. I wanted to know if you would like to have dinner and go to a movie this evening, if you are not too busy?"

"That sounds good; about what time do I need to be ready?"

"I'll say about six. I think that we are going to have a little bit of a late night. I should get you home about midnight, if that is not too late for you, for a work night? Dress causal, we're going to have a little fun tonight."

"I don't know if I'm ready for your kind of fun Jordan, but I can't resist, so I'll be ready and waiting for you."

Six o'clock and there's Jordan pulling in the driveway, on time as always. He is going to be so mad that I have to go away for two weeks with the firm. We are just going to have fun tonight, and think about tomorrow later. She thought to herself.

"Hey Baby, see I'm ready like I told you I would be. Thanks again for the balloons and flowers, I loved them. You made it hard to keep my mind on work and not on you. Before we go I have something for you." She went down the hall and came back with a small bag in her hand. "Happy Valentine's day"

"Tiffany, you didn't have to." Inside was a box containing a brushed silver chain bracelet on the back engraved were the words I LOVE YOU NOW AND FOREVER, TIFFANY. "Tiffany this is . . . . Are you sure? Thank you, I love it." They kissed.

"Hey! Hey, we have to get out of here, before we wind up not leaving at all. Let me get my coat."

Driving down the street Jordan turned to Tiffany and smiled. "I thought tonight we would shoot some pool and play darts. Do you know how to play?"

"Darts, I can play. Pool is another story, but you know I'm up for the challenge. What are we going to eat, I'm hungry?"

"We can eat there because they have the best chicken wings." He said smiling at Tiffany. "What . . . What, you were wanting hugging and kissing in a corner booth kind of Valentine's Day dinner? Not happening. This is going to be a win a game and you can eat kind of dinner and night. I hope you're up for it?"

"Looks like you are going to be hungry tonight, because I don't intend to loose." she said rubbing his leg as he turned into the parking lot.

*   *   *

"Okay bring on the food, I'm up three games to your one in darts, and I am ready to eat." She said cockily removing the darts from the board.

The waitress came to the table about fifteen minutes later bringing them their honey mustard and barbeque chicken wings and fries. "Here they are, you can eat now my queen. Dinner is served. Don't get too full, we still have to play some pool. Michael and Susan are coming so I hope you don't mind. I know the last time we were all together you kind of stole the show with your moves." Jordan chuckled "You said you don't know how to play pool right?"

"Michael and Susan are coming, this is going to be fun, and no I don't know how to play. So don't try and cheat me, got it."

"Here they are, hey Michael, Susan. The waitress should be back soon with some beers I ordered because I knew you guys would be here soon. Help yourself to the chicken wings and French fries."

"Okay rack them up! Let's get this game started. Tiffany we'll let you break."

Tiffany grabs a pool cue and aims pulls back and lets go of the stick, and it lands on the board. "Okay maybe someone else should break." Tiffany said laughing.

Jordan comes up behind her. "Okay this is how you need to hold the stick and bend down like this, and line the stick up with the ball you want to hit, pull back a bit and go." The balls went all over the board and even a few in the holes. "You did good Baby, real good."

"You two love birds need to get a room; we are here to play pool, darts and eat not to watch the two of you making out." Susan said picking up a piece of chicken.

The evening went on for hours, "Baby, I really need to get home, it's almost one in the morning and I have to go to work tomorrow. I know I'm being the party pooper, but I really need to go and get to bed." Tiffany said with a sad puppy dog look on her face. "Michael and Susan, see you next time. Besides Jordan aren't you tired of loosing every game to me yet?"

"On that man, we're out of here. Talk to you later bro and Susan I will be over for dinner sometime soon."

They got in Jordan's truck and headed for Tiffany's, "Jordan tonight was great. Not to put a downer on the night, but on Monday I will be leaving for two weeks with the senior accounting group, traveling to meet with some of our sister companies that we have major accounts with. At least I will be here on Saturday for my birthday and we can spend it together."

"Tiff a whole two weeks? They don't do this kind of thing often, do they?" Jordan said with a pain staking crushed look on his face.

"Relax, they don't, but you can meet me in some of the cities if you like and spend the night and hang out when I'm not in meetings if you're not too busy here?"

"I know I won't be able to do that on such short notice, but I can give you something to think about before you go. I want you to be able to go places and do things without you worrying about me and without me worrying about you. It's called trust and if this is going to work that's one of the main things that we're going to have to have. I love you and I mean that with all my heart. Just remember Saturday is mine all mine to be with you." kissing her as they stood on her front porch.

"Dad's keeping the kids for me this weekend, and for the two weeks I'll be gone. So this weekend I'll be all yours." she kissed him softly on the lips. "Have a good night with sweet dreams of me." She winked those big brown eyes at him.

Chapter 14

● ● ● ● ● ● ● ● ● ● ● ● ● ● ● ● ●

T he phone rang, waking Tiffany up from her sleep. "Good morning and happy birthday Tiff, I just called because I wanted to be the first person to wish you happy birthday and to see when I could come over and make you breakfast and make you happy."

"Well I am about to jump in the shower and then get dressed. How soon can you be here?"

"Just say the word and the time."

"Okay then right now to join me in the shower. How about that?" she said giggling. Just then she heard the door bell ring. No it couldn't be, she thought. She opened the door and Jordan was standing there handsome and sexy as ever.

"Like I said, your wish is my command." he replied licking his lips. "Once, again happy birthday, I have a gift for you out in the car, but you have to wait. Do you want me to start breakfast or do you need me to help you out in the shower?" He said biting his bottom lip.

"I'll let you decide." As she walks down the hall to her room the bath rode that she was wearing made its way to the floor just as she was turning the corner to go in the bedroom. She turned her head and winked at him.

"Guess I got my answer." as he started removing his coat and clothes to join her.

"Can I blow out my birthday candle or will I get in trouble?" she says as she started to rub the front of his boxers. "Slow down Baby, remember this is your day." as he moved her hand and pulled her closer to him they kissed, she opens her mouth and allowed his tongue to come in. She let a soft moan escape, as she tilts her head to the side as he began kissing her neck and cupped her breast in his hands, then moved down and began sucking and teasing them with his tongue one at a time making sure they had the same amount of attention given to both of them, he traveled down further as her moans got deeper, he starts by blowing cool breath on her and rubbing her. "Oh Jordan" escapes her lips as she grabs his shoulders and massages them as she moves her body in a grinding motion in his mouth; sucking her most intimate part and running his fingers in and out of her until she grabbed his shoulders and released herself with a loud moan, he then sealed it with a kiss and lick to top it off.

"Let me get some breakfast started. I'll be right back." As he stood up a patted her on the butt, all she could do was lay there in the middle of her bed and nod her head to agree.

Jordan returned shortly with an apron on and a tray in his hands with two plates with sausage, eggs and pancakes and two glasses of milk. "Good morning breakfast is now being served."

"Oh, this looks good." as she sat up on the bed.

"Are you talking about me or the food?"

"I'm talking about both, definitely both." Tiffany said licking her lips.

"After breakfast we are going to get in the shower, go shopping, the movies, and lunch and then . . . . like I told you I have a surprise for you."

"I like surprises, let me go and get in the shower and get ready." When she was out of the shower she put on a pair of jeans that hugged every long lean inch of her legs and a pair of riding boots, and a red sweater. She pulled her hair back with a black head band; she turned around and looked at Jordan sitting on the bed admiring the view. "Just wait till tonight when I return the favor to you." She said raising her eye brow.

"Let's get on our way with a day of shopping." Jordan said wrapping an arm around her waist and heading for the door.

At the mall they went to several stores, he purchased four outfits for her trip, lingerie for the evening, a swim suit that he told her not to wear until she got back home, and it was summer and they were alone and some of her favorite perfume. "You are spoiling me. I am not saying I don't like it, but man you need to stop. It's one o'clock, what time does this movie start?"

"It starts at three thirty. Let's get something to snack on, because I don't want to get too full now or at the movies because we are going some place really nice to eat later."

"Well in that case, let's continue shopping."

After the movies they headed back to Tiffany's to change clothes. She put on that little black dress the one that no woman should be without, and combed her hair in a way that it seductively fell over one eye with just a little hint of makeup, and three inch black stiletto pumps that had a strap around her ankles.

"That dress fits you nice and you look good. Are you ready to get something to eat?" Jordan said walking around her looking her up and down.

"I can say the same for you too, with the black pants and gray button down shirt, tie and that black Kangol hat tilted to the side, you make me want to skip dinner and keep you right here in my bed with me." as she grabbed him and planted a hard kiss on his lips.

"Cut it out. Where's your coat, we have reservations at six thirty and we are not going to be late." He pulled into the parking lot of Lee Lee's a five star restaurant that took weeks in advance to get reservations to. They were seated in the corner near a window with a candle burning in the center of the table.

A young waiter came over to the table, "Can I get your evening started with something to drink?"

"Yes we would like two glasses of red wine and two glasses of water. When you come back we should be ready to order. Thank you." As the waiter left the table he looked up, "Tiffany you look so beautiful tonight. How could I have ever been so stupid not to see it when I had it before?"

"Jordan we were young and we didn't know. You didn't know. If I've not told you already, thank you for all of the gifts and everything today. You have really made this a day to remember."

"Baby the nights not over yet. The best is yet to come. Here comes the waiter, do you know what you are going to have this evening?"

"Yes I think I will have the lobster, steak medium well, baked sweet potato and salad with French dressing."

"You know I think I'll have the same."

During dinner they laughed and talked and enjoyed each others company.

"Can I get any dessert for you this evening?" The waiter asked when he came and cleared the table.

"I'll have some strawberry cheesecake." Tiffany answered

"I'm fine, we just have to make her happy on her birthday. So whatever she wants." Jordan said.

The waiter came back to the table with the cheesecake.

"Oh my goodness it's so big. I'll never be able to eat all of this." Jordan moved his chair closer into the table and picked up her spoon and took a big scoop of cheesecake and fed it to her from across the table.

"I can't believe I ate the whole thing. Can you?"

"That just means that you are going to have to work it all off tonight. You ready to go?"

Arriving at her house that evening they pulled in the driveway. "Baby, why don't you go in, and get comfortable. I need to get something out of the trunk, and I'll be right behind you."

As she was taking her coat off, Jordan came up behind her and started kissing her neck. "Are you ready for your last gift?"

"Jordan, no you have gotten me too much already. I don't need anything else honestly." she said turning around looking him in the eyes.

"This is something that I should have given you years ago. Now that I have the chance again, I'm not going to blow it or put it off any longer." He got down on one knee in front of her in the foyer and took her by the hand. "Tiffany you were in my life years back, and I blew it by letting my hormones rule my thoughts and heart. I let not only you get away from me, but our son as well, and that is something that I will never forgive myself for. I just want you to know that I never truly stopped loving you. Instead of getting down on yourself and me, you grew. You went out on your own and had our son, went back to school and grew. Baby I don't want you to have to work that hard by yourself anymore. I want to be part of your life I want you to be my wife and be with me through thick and thin till death do us part. I want us to love each other through good and bad times . . . . Through the hard times, through the times when it hurts and the pain is so great but we love and get through it together. That's what I want and that is what I know we can be together, love true love. Tiffany Morgan will you marry me?" as he pulls out a small gift box from his pants pocket and opens it and shows her a beautiful emerald cut diamond solitaire set in white gold ring.

"I can't believe this Jordan, it's beautiful. Yes! Yes I love you so much Jordan. I would be honored to be your wife", she took his hand and pulls him up to her.

He takes the ring out of the box and places it on her finger. "Perfect fit." he says kissing her hand.

Tiffany led Jordan back to her bedroom, where she was going to give a little present of her own to enjoy. "Hey Jordan can you help me with this zipper. I think it's stuck?" turning her back to him so that he could help her.

As he started to unzip the back of her dress, he noticed the surprise that he was unveiling, under her dress she had on a black lacy bra with matching barely there panties and black thigh highs that had his heartbeat and his manhood rising to see more as the dress she was wearing hit the floor and she stepped over it still wearing her black stilettos. "You had your turn earlier today pleasing me and now it's my turn to return the favor." Pulling him close to her to steal a kiss before she got started on the real objective that was just below his belt, but she wanted him completely naked, starting with his tie slowly unbuttoning his shirt to expose his chest she could see his heart beating in his chest, which left her a little breathless. "Calm down we are just getting started." She said and went around to his back so that she could admire his strong broad shoulders, massaging them as she reached around to the front of him and began undoing his belt and unzipping his pants they fell to the floor as she walked back around to the front of him kissing him all the while. She could tell by the rise in his boxers that he was ready, she dropped down to her knees massaging him with her hands and soon her mouth was getting jealous by the way he was responding to the touch of her hands, her lips began to kiss him soon her tongue began massaging the very tip, letting him enjoy the texture of her tongue around the head of his penis, then she would stop and allow him to go in and out of her mouth, then slowing down to let her tongue massage him again.

"Yes Baby that feels so good. Oh Tiffany baby, yes, you're the best!" By his response that made her want to work even harder to please him by allowing her mouth to continue on with the dance that Jordan was so happily enjoying until finally he was done. "Baby you are so sexy. Don't take any of that off. I want you next to me just like that until I get my strength back and can take it off in my way." They lay in bed holding each other until about one in the morning when Jordan removed her remaining clothes and gave her a reason to sleep a little more in his arms.

The next morning Tiffany woke up on cloud nine, not only was she planning for a two week business trip but now a wedding. She knew that with Jordan around at least one of the jobs would be easy. "Good morning Baby breakfast is ready." as she carried a breakfast tray to him in bed.

"You are going to make me fat with all of this food. You know that don't you?"

"Don't worry, I'll still love you. So have you thought about a date for us to get married yet? You know I was thinking of purple, my favorite color along with lavender and black as our wedding colors. I think it should be a fall wedding? What do you think?"

"Okay September, October or November what do you think, your choice?" Jordan said in response.

"Let's go with October, that way we will have a little time to plan and get everything together. I don't want a big wedding either around a hundred to hundred and fifty guest. What do you think about that?"

"October is great."

"Okay then you have to pick the date. What Saturday sounds good to you?"

Jordan rolled over and picked up the pocket calendar on Tiffany's night stand. "Well let's see how about October seventh?"

"No because the kids are just getting back into school. Let's make it October twenty second? You can have the wedding as big or as small as you want it. We could even go downtown next week if that's what you said you wanted to do."

"I like the twenty second of October with all the fall colors. That would be nice."

"That sounds good Tiff."

"Then a fall wedding in purple it will be," as he pulled her down on the bed and kissed her. "Tiffany, have I told you this morning that I love you, because I do. Now we need to get on the phone and call the kids, your dad and Michelle and my mom and brother." He stopped and looks her in the eyes. "Tiffany I have something I want to ask you."

"No. don't say anything to mess this moment up Jordan."

"It's nothing bad, at least I don't think so. After we get married can we try and have one more baby? I know you have your career and you're doing things, but I would love to have another baby with you, so I can show you how good of a father I can be from day one."

"Wow Jordan, you keep on adding to my plate don't you? Let's be married for a few years at least one before we try, deal? You know I transferred into the accounting group from Virginia and they gave me a senior manager position with that transfer, so I don't want to get the position then come in a few months later and be pregnant. Plus I think a few of the guys don't like me because of that anyway. They feel like they deserved it more than I did. They feel that they put more time in, even though I have been with the company seven years just in another state, and worked my ass off just like them."

"Wait a minute, do I need to go in your office and take care of some bad attitudes and get them thinking and acting right?" He laughs "Baby I'm just joking with you. I know you have it under control. I can wait; I just needed to know that the door was open for me to come in. You know all this wedding and baby planning talk takes a lot out of a man. Do you want to take the part that's not worn out and show me what you can do with it?", as he kisses Tiffany and pulls her down next to him in bed.

"Wait a minute Jordan; let's slow this down just a little. I think we should wait until our honeymoon before we have sex again. I know that we already have a kid together and that we have already made love, and been having sex but I just want to wait and make it special not just another night of sex that we have been doing all along."

"Mmmmm . . . . So no more sex until we get married, right?" He sat up and looks at Tiffany with a look to said, you're just playing right?

"Jordan, don't get me wrong, I love you I just want this to be right. Sex can be good even great for a few months, but we need to know that there is more to us than that. We need to know we can talk, enjoy and love each other without making love. Do you think that's going to be a problem? I want to be Mrs. Jordan Alexander more than you know. We're going to do this and it is going to work. Trust me, better yet trust us." she said kissing him on the lips.

"Okay Tiff, I trust us. We can do this. Let's get up and get our day going, because if we keep lying here, we will have to start the "No sex" thing tomorrow. Just promise me, the lingerie I just got you, I want to see that on you October twenty second, now is that a deal? Speaking of that, where do you want to go on our honeymoon anyway so I can see that?"

"Let's see I have never been to Hawaii or Jamaica . . . .

"You pick, I have been to both places."

"Hmmm . . . . both places, well then it looks like Hawaii in October."

"Hawaii it is then. Are you sure you want to wait until October before we can . . . .", and Jordan wrapped his arms around her and pulled in close to him.

"Stop Jordan." she pulls away from his embrace. "We are not going to make till October if you keep doing things like this."

"Okay! Okay! You can't blame a man for trying, getting and seeing all that and then knowing what we did just a few hours ago. I know Tiff, I'll be good, beside don't we have to start getting you all packed for your two week business adventure?"

"Let's get up shower, and get a dressed, separate shower that is, because I can't handle all of that." Looking at Tiffany laid across her bed with her robe just barely covering her legs, and the treasure that was between them.

Chapter 15

● ● ● ● ● ● ● ● ● ● ● ● ● ● ● ● ● ● ●

Monday morning came around quickly, and the ride to the airport was quiet. "I gave you names of the cities and the hotel numbers and the dates that we'll be at each one, didn't I? Just think Jordan, I wont have to do this again until next year. Two weeks is nothing, I'll back here and we'll be planning the wedding in no time."

"I know sweetheart, it's just that I'm asking so much of you, I don't want you to run away. I mean we're back in one another's lives again and I don't want anything or anybody to come between us again. So Dallas, Texas first for two days right, then Houston for two days then . . . ."

"Then I will be calling you and missing you everyday that we're apart. Jordan stop it, I love you and I want to be Mrs. Jordan Alexander and we're going to be together until we are both old and gray sitting on the front porch swinging talking about our grandkids. I love you baby with everything I have and feel." Tiffany kissed her hand and placed it on his lips, then rubs his shoulder never letting her eyes leave his face.

"I know you do and I love you too Tiff." returning a glance in her eyes before turning back around to focus on the road. "We should be at the airport in about thirty minutes and your plane should be leaving the airport about thirty minutes after that."

"I got your bags; you just grab what you are taking on the plane with you."

Tiffany turned around and got her carry-on bag out of the trunk. "Oh there's another one of the senior partners, Gary Smith, he thinks he does it all by himself and that we all should just shut up and listen to everything he says and follow everything he does. Most of the time he smells of alcohol and forgets half the things he says including the clients names." Tiffany turned and put her brief case strap over her shoulder, then turns back around. "Good morning Gary, glad to see you made it through all this weather. I think the plane is already here. Gary this is my fiancée Jordan Alexander, Jordan this is one of the senior management people Gary Smith. It looks like everyone else is already heading to board the plane." Tiffany turns and kisses Jordan softy on his lips." I love you Jordan. This time is going to go by quicker then you, I mean then we think."

Jordan leans over and whispers in Tiffany's ear, "I love you to Tiff, and I want you to knock them out and show them who the boss really is."

$*$ $*$ $*$

They had two cars waiting at the airport when they arrived in Dallas to take them to the hotel. At the hotel she went to the front desk and got checked into her room. When she opened the door to her room tears started rolling down her face when she saw the bouquet of flowers next to the television, they were from Jordan, with a card that said, "I LOVE YOU AND I AM GOING TO MISS YOU, JORDAN"

Tiffany took out her cell phone and dialed Jordan's number and his voice mail picked up. "Jordan you are going to make two weeks seem like years if you keep doing things like this. The flowers are lovely. I made it here safely. I miss you and love you too. I'll talk to you later. Stop by and tell the kids mommy misses them and I'll be back before they can even get a chance to miss me too much." she left the message then hung up the phone.

Just then a knock came on the door; she looked though the peep hole. It was Bill from the office. What could he want? Tiffany opened the door. "What can I do for you, Bill?"

"Can I come in Tiffany? I'm holding up a truss flag." Bill said holding up a hanker chief and waving it in the air.

"Come in. What can I do for you?" Tiffany said moving to the side to allow him in.

"Well for starters, I just wanted to tell you that I was sorry for acting like an ass when you gave me the opportunity to go out with you. I said some pretty hurtful things to you and I just wanted to tell you that I was sorry. Tell Jordan that I apologize to him as well. He's a very lucky man, but if he ever gives you any problems remember you can always call me and I'll be there, because you are an incredible woman. I'm glad I got the chance to tell you this and again I am sorry for everything before."

"Well thank you Bill and I'll be sure and tell Jordan what you said. Don't be holding your breath about that call, because I . . . . or should I say we're not changing our minds or hearts about one another ever again."

"He's a lucky man, that's all I have to say. You want to go down stairs and get something to eat?"

"Okay, I hear the food here is good. Let me just grab my purse."

After dinner Bill made the suggestion for the two of them to go back to his room for a night cap.

"Bill like I told you and have been telling you all night, thanks for the apology but I love Jordan and I don't need any other men."

Bill leaned back in his chair and held up his hands. "You can't blame a man for trying? On that note I guess I will drop you off at your room and say good night."

* * *

Each city and state they went to, a bouquet of flowers was always in the hotel room waiting for her to arrive. By the end of the two weeks Tiffany was tired of being tired and ready to be home and sleeping in her own bed.

The time flew by quickly getting ready for the wedding and all of the wedding plans.

"Tiffany what do you want to do for Labor Day?"

"We can have a pool party and get ready to close down the pool for the year. Invite some family and friends over and you can fix your world famous bar-b-cue and I will take care of the side dishes, and if people want they can bring something and just have fun in the pool. The weather is supposed to be good. What do you say?"

"That sounds good to me, and I am glad you realize my skill on the grill. We can put some corn on the cob on there to along with the meat."

*   *   *

"Jordan, good morning. What time are you coming over to start cooking? I have already started cooking my part of the meal."

"I have all the meat marinating, so all I'll have to do is fire up the grill and begin. I got the hot dogs, chicken wings, brats, ribs and burgers just waiting for my grilling skills to make it finger licking good. I should be over in about an hour."

"Well I have you beat then because I already have the potato salad, pasta salad, fruit salad, and baked beans already done. So I will be able to just sit back and watch you cook and I can go swimming. See you when you get here." Tiffany said so seductively over the phone.

"Mmmmm . . . Your voice. Just remember one more month and you are all mine to have, to hold, love and cherish for the rest of our lives. And I will love you for the rest of our lives till death do us part. See you in a little bit Tiff."

* * *

Later that evening after everyone was full from food and worn out from swimming, dancing and game playing and everyone had decided to go home. Tiffany went in the house to check on the kids to find them already asleep in their beds; she turned out the lights in their rooms, turned off the TV's, and closed the doors. She went back out by the pool to join Jordan who was still bursting with energy and ready to swim laps around the pool.

"Can I get you something else to drink while I finish cleaning up out here?"

"Yeah. What can I do to help you Tiff?"

"Anything you see, just jump on in and do what ever you see that needs to be done. I'll be right back with the drinks." she went in the house and came back out with two long island ice teas. "I hope it's not too strong for you?"

"Oh girl, you would make anyone happy as a bartender." He said taking a small sip out of his glass.

"After we clean up, do you want to go for a swim before I head home?"

"Why not." she took her rode off after they finished, and there she stood with a white one piece swim suit on that covered the curves just enough to enjoy everything that it didn't.

"I love that birthday present on you, I picked a good one." Jordan said admiring the view in front of him.

"That you did. I like it too." She said with a flirtatious smile.

Before jumping into the pool Tiffany bent over to get some grass off of her foot. Jordan looked over and saw her shapely legs and perfectly rounded ass and breast as round and firm as freshly harvested melons all of that in one month would be all his to have and to hold and his soldier stood at attention, as she jumped into the pool, and Jordan quickly joined her. Swimming up behind her put his arms around her, she stopped and stood up in the middle of the pool, Jordan swam up next to her for a kiss. "I love you Tiff." and began kissing her again. "You taste good and look good too. I don't want to let you go." they began kissing more passionately. "Tiffany if we don't stop, I won't be able to."

"I am not stopping you, Jordan." She said looking into his eyes.

That is all he needed to hear, he pulled Tiffany to the side of the pool, and sat down on the step inside the pool and Tiffany moved over on top of him. He moved her swimsuit over to the side and enters her, slowly she moved up and down filling herself with him until he was done and she had been satisfied as well.

"I'm sorry Tiffany, I couldn't help myself. I know that we both agreed to wait, but baby I . . . ."

"Relax Jordan; it was just as much me to. I have been holding out and wanting you every time I see you, every time I think about you and tonight I just couldn't stop myself. Its okay one month and we'll be Mr. and Mrs. Jordan Alexander. It's okay, let's get out of here before we get started again." as she splashes water in his face. "Man cool off, you are making me hot."

"I got a hose that can put your fire out for the night, if you like." holding her close enough to feel what he was offering. "Let me quit, come on let's get out of here. I need to get home so that I can take a cold shower and dream about holding you and doing all of the things that we like doing together." as he licks his lips with anticipation as his eyes looked her up and down. Then took her by the hand to help her out of the pool, once out of the pool they began kissing again. "Okay, okay I love you, but now it's time we slow down and give it a rest for the night. I'm going in the house and putting some clothes on and then I'm going to get out of here and I'll see you in the morning my love."

"You're right Jordan, go in and get dressed and we'll see each other tomorrow." she picked up the glasses they just had and headed in the house.

*   *   *

"What's going on with you today Jordan, because it's October first and the girls and I are getting together for the final fitting of our dresses and then we are all going out to lunch, and I am going to give them their gifts for being in the wedding. It's just going to be a fun day with the girls."

"Are you feeling better, I know last night you were saying that you did not feel well. Me and the fellas are going to catch a college football game out of town then go out to dinner and just hang out for a bit, but if we are too full then we are going to just get a room and come back in the morning. Did Susan ask if she could stay in the guest room tonight? You know she doesn't like being in that big house by herself since it's so far out."

"Yes I am feeling better, thanks for asking. Susan and I already worked everything out, and before we go to the final fitting, she is going to bring her overnight bag to the house and I think that we are going to ride together wherever we go. You know safety in numbers. I guess that means that I will see you tomorrow sometime."

"You never know, I just might come slipping in your bed tonight, to hold you and keep you warm, and throw Michael in the other room with Susan."

"Stop, you can come over if you want, but you have to sleep on your own side of the bed, and you know Michael is more than welcome to come and be with Susan."

"Speaking of rooms and houses, I saw the perfect house for us. Five bedrooms, four of them upstairs and the master bedroom downstairs and a finished basement, a sun room, and four bath rooms two on the main level, one upstairs and one in the basement, a pool in the backyard, a three car garage, and to top it off, a work shop in a backyard garage. I want you to see it next week sometime and tell me what you think."

"It sounds nice, and big. I like that plus that master bedroom down stairs and the pool? Oh yeah that sounds nice. Susan and I can drive by and see it today. What's the address?"

"Calm down Tiffany, we will see it together next week. I want to see your face and know what you really think about it first hand."

"No fair, but I'll wait. I'll see you either tonight or in the morning sometime."

*　　*　　*

"Susan, I didn't think you would ever get here. You got rid of Michael and Jordan, because I know the two of them probably drove you crazy getting out of your house this morning. Did you remember your bag? I'll show you where the guest room is."

"You know those two guys are like big kids. You know whatever happened with you and Jordan all those years ago, I'm glad that the two of you worked it out, because that man would move heaven and earth if you asked him to. It's love and nothing but love. You two look almost as good as me and Michael." as she laughed and patted Tiffany on the shoulder as she went into the guest room. The guest room had a queen size bed against a wall, the walls were an off white eggshell shade, the comforter was brown and tan kind of like drifting sand on an ocean front was spread across the bed, in the corner was a mahogany chest of drawers that sat against the wall and a mirrored dresser with a night stand next to the bed and flat screen TV mounted to the wall. "This room is really nice, and I love all the natural colors, it just makes you feel all warm and welcome coming in. I know I will sleep good in here tonight."

"Jordan told me this morning that he has found a house that he wants me to see. By the way he was describing it, it sounds perfect. This house is nice, but he is talking about another baby. I told him that after we were married for a year or so we would try, so I guess he feels that we need a bigger house so that we can have plenty of room and we are not waiting till the last minute to find one. He would not give me the address but he told me that we could see it together next week, because he wants to see my face when I see it."

"You two are amazing together, if he picked it out, you will love it because you know all he was thinking about when he found it was you. You guys got that . . . . I can't even put it into words. You know that till death do us part vibe and truly be happy."

"Michelle, Julie, Felicia and Amanda should be here shortly and I think that we are only going to take two cars. So we'll all be together. We are going to be able to bring our dresses home today unless they need more work. I am not even taking any chances I'm giving my dress to Michelle to take home, where I know Jordan's eyes can't see it, because you know he is too noisy."

"Oh there's the door bell." Tiffany says heading to the door. "Good we are all here now let's get going. We are going to have a ball, no guys' just all ladies hanging out all day. This is going to be fun, let's get out of here."

"Jordan is going to fall in love all over again once he sees you in that dress . . . It looks a little more form fitting then when you first tried it on. Did they take a little too much up in the mid section? Don't forget take it easy taking that off, because we don't want it ripped, besides that it's is going in my closet. Like you, and I both know Jordan is noisy, and he ain't getting in mine and your father's bedroom before your wedding to look in closets." Michelle said holding up a hanger for Tiffany to hang the dress on.

"Yes Mama Michelle, I will make sure it is yours until the twenty second."

Tiffany began to take the lavender wedding gown off; the other girls looked at how it was fitting so perfectly every single inch. "I'm starving, when are we going to get something to eat?"

"Girl you keep eating the way you have been, people are going to start to think you're pregnant, and that wedding dress you're going to have to put a stretch band in the waist band of it just to fit on your big day.", Felicia chimed in and said causing all the girls to look at Tiffany for a yes or no answer to the pregnancy question.

"Get out of here, I'm not pregnant. We planned on having another kid in about a year but no sooner because of my job. What you want to go down the street and buy a pregnancy test to see for yourself?"

"I got a ten, because I want to know. You know satisfy my curiosity. Let's go they have a drug store just over there." Amanda said waving her ten dollar bill in the air.

"Okay let's go get the test and then we'll get something to eat and we'll go to my house and take the test so I can prove to you guys that you just wasted your money." Tiffany said as she snatched the ten dollar bill out of Amanda's hand.

Tiffany and Susan road back together after lunch, Susan turned around and looked at Tiffany, "Is there a possibility that you're pregnant? I know you said that you and Jordan were going to wait until after the wedding, but sometimes things happen."

"I told Jordan on my birthday back in February when he asked me to marry him that I wanted to wait until our wedding night before we had sex again. Then last month on labor day when we had people over and after everyone left, we were playing around jumped in the pool, kissing and the next thing you know making love without any kind of protection, so yes there is a chance." Tiffany confessed as she put her head in her hands.

"It's not a bad thing, I mean the two of you both work, you are getting married anyway, and you are looking at a bigger house to move into. What's wrong with filling it up a little quicker than planned? You love each other it would be that bad? Come on the rest of the ladies are pulling up behind us, and we all want to know. You said you had to go to the bathroom anyway? Let's go." Susan said as Tiffany grabbed the bag with the pregnancy test in it. "I need to go to my car and get something, I'll meet you inside."

Tiffany saw the other ladies putting their dresses in their cars and remember that she had not given them their wedding party gifts, so she grabbed them from her trunk and brought the gifts inside with her.

"Hey baby, are you okay? You don't have to do this. We can all go home and you can do this in private. Then call me and tell me the results." Michelle said hugging her as if to reassure her that everything was going to be okay. "Let me go and put my mother's dress in the car and I'll be right in, okay sweetie?"

"Thanks mama Michelle, I know you're right. I just feel like I did when I was a teenager and brought a pregnancy test when I found out that I was pregnant with Kendall. I just don't know how I feel about history repeating itself."

"I can get the girls and we can go and you can do this by yourself if you want. Just tell me and we'll do whatever you want."

"I need all you guys here, but I'm not so sure I'm not worried about what the results are going to be."

* * *

"Let's get this party started! Tiffany you go down the hall and take that little test and we will turn on some music and get a card game started. Does anyone feel lucky tonight?" Amanda said fanning herself with a deck of cards.

"I'll be right back; I have been holding it for too long now." Tiffany said turning on the light in the bathroom and closing the door behind her.

"Let's get it all set up now. You got the cake out of your car Felicia? We got all of the gifts out too, I just wish Jordan's mom could have been able to come, but you know she is always traveling. Will she be here on their wedding day?" Julie said sarcastically

"Yes I got the cake out of the car, so stop being a smart ass! I know that Tiffany and Jordan sent his mom an invitation, but you all know that her brother has been sick. I think that's what Tiffany told me. I don't think he is doing that good at all, but you know that Jordan is her oldest son and she is glad that he is finally with a woman that is going to treat him right and now possibly give her more grandbabies. Oh . . . . You know Tiffany will be number one with her again, since she missed out on so many years of Kendall not being right there for her to spoil" Felicia said

"I guess I probably shouldn't offer Tiffany a drink if she's pregnant huh . . . . ?" Amanda said pouring herself a glass of wine.

"Shut up, let her find out first. Then we will go from there." Michelle chimed in.

"That sucks not being able to drink on your own wedding day, and then having to put up with some man climbing all over you flipping this way and that, doing whatever he wants to until he gets tired. Get drunk I say then you will never know what he's done and it will be all over with, but for a little soreness down there." Amanda with that look of disgusted on her face.

"What kind of man are you married to? That sounds disgusting! You guys need to get some counseling or something." Felicia said rolling her eyes and frowning up her face.

"I got it all together." Julie said.

"Surprise!" they all yelled as Tiffany came walking down the hall.

"Surprise is right, I'm pregnant!" Tiffany looked around the room to see everyone's reaction to the news.

"Congratulations girl, you love that man and he loves you. What difference does it make if it is a little sooner than the one or two years down the road you planned? Planning things like this is too over rated. Things like this just happen so be happy. Beside that Jordan's a good man." Julie said reaching out to give Tiffany a hug.

"Don't get me wrong, I am happy. I'm just surprised that's all. I wonder what Jordan's going to say?" Tiffany said as a tear rolled down her cheek.

"Stop that, he's going to be happy and we'll have to pull him down off of cloud nine and you know it." Michelle said. "Your father is going to be probably just as happy as Jordan and riding on a cloud right next to him."

Tiffany wiped the tears from her face. "Wait a minute, I've got gifts for each of you for being in my wedding and helping me out with everything. I want you to wear them the day of the wedding, they go with the dresses, and I'm going to be wearing one too."

"This is kind of like a bridal party, because we have some gifts for you too, but no strippers, sorry." Michelle said smiling.

The ladies drank, ate food like there was no tomorrow, played card games and other games, told stories about what happens when the lights go out in their houses with their men, some where giving too much detail and some girls not knowing what to do when the lights went out to keep your man happy advice. Mama Michelle just kept saying love him and do your best for you and your man and your kids and things will work out, whatever you are going through. She also said that all of the sex in the world could not make a marriage or keep a marriage happy if real love is not there, and to also keep God in your heart and he will guide you and direct you and keep you.

"Okay I hate to kick all of you guys out, but we have been here for hours and it almost one o'clock in the morning and we all have Church in the morning. I want to thank you all for the gifts and for all of your help and support getting me ready for my special day. And yes I will be telling Jordan first thing in the morning if not tonight. If they get back in town, so when you see him tomorrow at Church, he should already know. Thank you guys once again, you've been great." Tiffany said smiling.

Chapter 16

● ● ● ● ● ● ● ● ● ● ● ● ● ● ● ● ●

Tiffany heard the front door open and Jordan and Michael trying to whisper walking down the hall. Jordan came in the room and sat down on the bed and began taking off his shoes. "I'm not asleep Jordan; you can turn on the light if you need to. I was just lying in here thinking." She said with a kind of cry in her voice.

"Tiff, it's almost three in the morning, are you alright?"

"Jordan, I have something to tell you."

"What's going on? What's wrong?"

"Turn on the lights; I want to see your face when I tell you this."

"Tiff, you are scaring me. Tell me what?" as he turns on the light and sat down next to her in the bed.

"Jordan I don't have all of the details yet, but I am thinking about in May we are going to have another addition to our family." she looked up at him waiting for a reaction.

"Oh my God Tiff, are you . . . . pregnant?" He looked at her with those warm chestnut brown eyes and a smile grew on his face looking at her. "Oh baby I love you, when did you find out? Have you gone to see the doctor yet? Let me guess, Labor Day in the pool that's when it happened right? Ohhhhhh baby . . . . that's good news right? I know you wanted to wait, but here we are."

"Yes, it was Labor Day and no I have not seen a doctor yet. On Monday I'll have to call and make an appointment with my doctor, and yes Baby this is good news." leaning over to kiss him.

"Baby that just means that this was meant to be, you, me, us and now a new baby under construction." Jordan said smiling rubbing her stomach.

"Stop, I haven't gotten that much bigger yet, but I know that I will probably start showing a lot sooner, since I already have had three kids."

"Tiff Baby, you are in better shape then most women that have not even had one kid yet. Just think of all of fun we are going to have working all of the weight off after the baby is born." Jordan said climbing on top of her looking her in the eyes and kissing her face until she started laughing and pushing him off.

"Stop Jordan you are so crazy."

He pulled back and slid off her. "If you are so happy about this, why were you lying here in the dark? I don't get it Tiff, are you sure your okay with this?"

"I was just thinking about the last time I found out that I was pregnant by you what happened. I know that we have only really been back together for a while and we are moving so fast, but I love it and I love you so much, I just didn't want to run you away with the news that I was pregnant. Then I saw your face . . . . your face said it all and more. It told me that you really want this baby and that makes me happy. Now I know for sure that we are doing the right thing by getting married." Tiffany said as tears started running down her cheeks.

"Tiffany I was a fool when we were younger, but I always wanted to know about Kendall from the day that you told me that you were pregnant, I just didn't know how to get in contact with you, and I promise you that I never even saw the letters that you mailed to the house and you said were returned to you unopened with return to sender on the envelope. Brooklyn was hot, and she saw that I was hurting and wanting to talk to you but she just kept coming by and soon she got to me. She was giving me everything that I thought you weren't which was time, sex and conversation. She was cheering me on in college when some guys from the NBA were coming out to see me, and then all of the sudden Brooklyn tells me she is pregnant and her mom said that we had to get married because her baby girl was not going to have a baby born out of wed lock, so we got married. Not even a big wedding, then the honeymoon she went all out of this world with spending money. When she finally figured out that I was not going to anyone's NBA team, she's not pregnant anymore. Now that should have been my first clue, nothing but a gold digger when she drank more than me the entire time we were gone on our honeymoon, and flirted her ass off with every man in the place that she thought had a dollar, then when we got back a week later the miscarriage, then the oh . . . . it hurts too bad when we have sex so we shouldn't do that for a while, then the trips out of town lasting for weeks and no call no nothing when she was gone, not even a number that I could call to talk with her or name or a number to a hotel where she was staying. Hell half the time I would not even know what city or state she would be in. I had also found out that you had gotten married and about Kendall to, so I was mad and my feelings hurt just to know that you fell in love with someone and it was not me and that you were happy, because your dad would come to Church and make announcements about you all of the time from the birth of Kendall, to your marriage, to your getting your degree, passing your CPA exam and to the birth of Jessica and Anna, yes your dad informed us of every step of your happy little life, and I was pissed off because I was not a part of it. I also knew that I should have been that man making and keeping you happy. So needless to say on those Sundays, I just went home pissed off and got nothing out of the sermon if I even heard the sermon at all that day. When I heard about what happened to David and that you were moving back home. I had to thank God that I might have another chance to show you that I could be better then the man you fell in love with all those years ago, and I'm never going to let you go. Don't get me wrong, I was sorry for you about David, but I was glad that I could possibly get another chance."

Words escaped her, but tears were coming down like rain. Jordan wiped her face and the two of them laid their holding each other in silence all night long.

*   *   *

"Good morning Baby and good morning to you too baby." Jordan said kissing her on the stomach right above her panty line. "That's about where we are at right?" rubbing on her stomach some more and looking up at Tiffany.

"Yes I guess, maybe not even that far up yet. Just enough to give me that bloated tummy look. I just hope I can keep it sucked in a bit longer, so I can fit into my wedding dress because it's too late for any alterations, but I think you will be happy with the dress and the way it looks."

"Tiffany, if you are in it then I know I'm going to love it, but before we go any further let me know just one thing for sure." he looked her in the eyes with the smile leaving his face. "Are you sure that you want to keep this baby? I know that you talked about your job, your new position and you are just getting settled back into town and you'll be walking down the isle soon. I don't want this just to be another thing to overwhelm you to have to deal with, just let me know your honest answer yes or no? Trust me baby I will understand either way." he laid still waiting for an answer just holding onto her hands.

"Jordan, I know I said that I wanted to wait a year after we were married . . . . But this little one is here and does not want to wait a year on mommy's job to makes it's little grand entrance. I know I just found out, correction we just found out, but this has to be right. It feels right, it feels good, and who are we to stop our miracle? It's right and yes we are going to have this baby." Jordan held onto her hands tightly and brought them up to his lips and kissed them.

"Thank you Baby, you don't know how much this means to me."

*   *   *

A knock came on the bedroom door, "Come on in." Jordan called out.

Susan and Michael came in "Hey bro congratulations, I hear there's another little Alexander on the way? Man couldn't you keep that thing in your pants until after the wedding? You know these boys are lethal when unleashed." Michael said rubbing his beard with his hand.

"Mike man if she was yours what would you do if left alone for five minutes?"

"Why do you think Susan and I have three kids? It's from being left alone, but bro don't brag about that five minute thing. That's not cool."

"Hey Susan and I are right here! Did you guys forget?" Tiffany said throwing a pillow at Jordan.

"And ahhh . . . . Michael just for the record, it's more then five minutes. Remember I'm your big brother. I taught you the techniques on how to please a real woman." putting his hand on his chin with that sexy smile shining through in Tiffany's direction. "Let's go down the hall and cook these women up some breakfast because you know they want to gossip, before you guys leave. I think I will take you by the house today." Jordan said leaving out and winking at Tiffany.

"So Tiffany, what did Jordan say when you told him?"

"I think he is happier than me. He was telling that me that I didn't have to keep the baby if I wasn't ready for one yet. Kissing my stomach and just making me feel like I was the queen of his world. You know, I just know that he's going to stick by me all of the way this time." Tiffany said looking at Susan and rubbing her stomach. "Now for my dad and the kids, I know they are going to be happy to, especially Kendall. Mommy and Daddy you did it again. Jessica and Anna will be happy only if they find out that this baby is a boy, so none of the little girly girl attention won't be taken off them"

"You're truly blessed girl. You have not only had the love from one man, but you've been in love and loved by two men. I know for a fact that Jordan loves you. I remember being in my bedroom when Jordan came over one night shortly after you had gotten back into town and he was telling how he wished that he had never messed up with you and that he would do anything to have a second chance with you, and how he would show you that he was a different man and that he was a real man and he would do his best never to hurt you again, because he missed out on so much already."

"He tells me those things, but when I think of yesterday. I just get real mad because he did miss out on so much time with me. Not to say that I would ever trade a minute of my life with David, but Jordan knew both of our lives would have been different if things would have happened differently. No one really knows what would have been different if things did not happen just the way they did. I know that I love him and he is the one I want to grow old with and yes the one I want to have and am going to have another child with." Tiffany stood up and put on her robe. "We better get down to the kitchen before they come looking for us, because they have it smelling wonderful already."

"Here, someone is on the phone wants to talk to you." Jordan hands Tiffany the phone with the receiver covered.

"Hello?" She says questionably

"Yes, dad it's true. You are going to be a Grandpa again, but I told Jordan I have to still go to the doctors and make sure everything is okay and figure out a possible date, but I will have more answers for everyone soon. I promise." She stood there just glowing listening to all of the advice from her father had to give her. She knew that this was going to be a special pregnancy for her father to since he would be able to see her from start until finish since with all her other babies she had been in Virginia and he was only able to see his grandchildren a few times a year.

"Yes Dad, I am more than okay. I don't think I could ask for anything more. We're going to look at a bigger house today. I couldn't be happier." Jordan came up behind her and wrapped his arms around her and kissed her on the back of the neck. "I'll see when we pick-up the kids about three. Love you too."

"You . . . . You need to stop that when I'm on the phone. You see what happens when the two of us get to close together." she said rubbing stomach and laughing.

"But baby you look so good how could I ever resist you?" looking at her with those sexy flirtatious eyes.

"So when do we get to go look at the house? Michael and Susan do you guys want to come see the house to? The more the merrier, plus the more eyes we have looking they can see if there are any questions that we should be asking about the house"

"That sound like a plan, since we don't have to pick up the kids until about three this afternoon?"

"That's right, so we have plenty of time, so let's all get cleaned up and go, we can make almost day out of it."

*　　*　　*

They pulled up in front of the house about an hour later, got out of Jordan's truck. Jordan got off his phone. "The realtor said that he would be here in about five minutes to show us the inside, but for now let's look around back."

They opened the gate to the backyard, "I love it already from the back yard alone. Look how big it is, look at the pool, it's perfect. I can't wait to see the inside. Oh Jordan, baby this house is . . . ."

"Hi, you must be the Alexander's? My name is Robert Brown, I'm with Good Homes Real Estate Agency." the man said as he extended he hand in Jordan's direction.

"Hello, my name is Jordan Alexander; this is my brother Michael and his wife Susan and my soon to be wife Tiffany.

"Good to meet everyone. Shall we get started with the tour of the house?" Robert said leading them from the back to the front of the house. The tour took about an hour looking at all of the rooms and imagining what would look good in each room all way to what color each room would be painted.. Robert gave them his business card and told them to call him if they had any questions.

"Jordan this house is perfect, I'm glad that we already went to the bank and got that part out of the way. We need to call and get the appraiser out and get the ball moving. I want to be in before the holidays, because with both of our houses we have a lot of the furniture already, just a few little things here and there and . . . ." Jordan kissed her.

"Stop . . . . stop talking for just a second, you are making me tired just listening to you. You see that bush right outside the master bedroom window? That's a lilac bush so in the spring when is starts blooming the sweet smell of lilac's will greet you at every sunrise and sunset. What do think about that?" he said biting his bottom lip, with a look like he planted it there himself to grow just for her.

"I'm ready to move in right now. I know where I want everything." looking like a little kid passing by the Christmas tree the days before Christmas seeing all the presents and just hoping that somehow one of them would just pop open so she could see.

"Okay I'll make some calls on Monday and get the ball rolling. Now let's get out of here and go find something to eat. What sounds good, anybody?"

After lunch the rest of the afternoon was spent playing spades girls against the guys back at Tiffany's until Michael and Susan went home to spend time with their kids and Tiffany and Jordan left to pick up the kids.

* * *

"October twenty second finally here, I can't believe I feel this nervous." Tiffany said looking into Mama Michelle's eyes for comfort.

"Everything is going to be okay. We just need to get you to the Church and dressed without you getting sick to your stomach again. Tiffany, you just need to calm down." Michelle said giving her a big hug. "Now your father will be in here real soon so stop all of that. You know Jordan loves you and those kids and he would do anything and everything for you. You have found a man as good as your father in my opinion. He's a good man baby so just relax."

The door opened up and Ken walked in. "Is everything okay with you girls? I got your dresses in the car and all of the other things you said that you needed. So let's get ready to get out of here." he looked over at Tiffany and could see that she was upset about something. "Hey Michelle can you give me a second?" Ken began to close the door to Tiffany's bedroom.

"Sure I'll be right in the front room" Michelle said and finished closing the door behind her.

"Come over here Tiffany. What seems to be the problem?" holding his daughter's hand as she began to cry.

"I don't know Dad. It's just my life, in a year and a half has been moving so fast. I just hope I'm not moving too fast into another relationship. Look at me now, I'm even pregnant. Dad . . . . don't get me wrong, I know I love Jordan, and you were right, he has grown and matured, and I do believe him when he tells me that he loves me, and that he wants to be with me. I don't know; I . . . . I guess butterflies. I want to know that this is going to be my happily ever after. I want to grow old with this man. You know, be that cute old couple walking in the park together holding hands or sitting on the front porch playing dominoes waiting for the kids and grandkids to come by and visit. You know like you and Michelle do. It hurts when forever is cut short, but you still have to learn to go on. You learned that from mom and me with David, it hurts. It hurts so bad, that you can't even think about tomorrow, or even getting out of bed, but you know that there is more than just you that you are living for and that they need your strength to help them get through. Now you have found Mama Michelle and the two of you look so good and so happy together. I just want the same for me and Jordan daddy." Her eyes began to pool up with water. "Oh I need to stop this; I am going to ruin my make-up. I love you Daddy. Thank you for always being there for me and your grandkids because I know at times we can be enough to make you want to loss your mind, but thanks for standing by us and just being there."

"We both know in life that seasons change, but we just have to grow and with God's help we make it through the cold winters in our life to prepare us for a fresh and new warmth of spring and summer to yet again face another winter, only this time a little bit better prepared. God will bless you with everything that you need to get through those seasons, just believe. He has always been there holding your hand and guiding you and keeping you strong, and you made it. Don't get me wrong, I'm not saying that you will never have times when you feel like everything and everyone has turned their backs on you and have left you all alone. In that moment, but don't turn from God, but hold on to Him even closer, and you will make it through and come back even stronger. Just look at you now, even stronger. Now come on we need to get out of here. We can't keep your husband to be and guest waiting. By the way, you look beautiful." Placing his hand under her chin and kissing her on the forehead. "Beautiful . . . . Tiffany, you are beautiful."

*   *   *

They went to the back of the Church where the other ladies had already gotten dressed and waiting for Tiffany's arrival. They rushed her in and began helping her get dressed and touched up her make-up and hair. A knock came on the door; first Mama Michelle came in followed by Ken. "They are ready for you. Are you girls all ready?" Ken said looking his baby girl.

"I'm ready Daddy." Tiffany said turning around looking at Ken dressed in his black tux.

"If I must say so again you look absolutely beautiful, you remind me of your mother the day the two of us were married. She had her father right at her side letting her know that she was marring a good man and that he would never give her away to someone that he knew would hurt her or break her heart. Now I believe that Jordan is that man and now he is man enough to be your husband and make you happy. He's a lucky man." Ken said taking her by the hand and headed to the center isle of the church.

The last bridesmaid was down the isle and off to the left side of the alter, the congregation stood as Ken and Tiffany stood in the doorway as Jordan began singing "Here and Now by Luther Vandross". Which gave Ken and Tiffany the cue to start their journey down the isle to join Jordan at his side in front of the alter. Jordan looked at Tiffany and fell in love with her all over again when he saw her. The lavender, slightly form fitting, full length dress, a single strand of pearls that were her mothers, that she had left her, graced her neck with earrings to match, her hair pulled up into a French role with curls softly dancing over her ears, make-up just enough to accent not to cover up anyone so perfect on this day and it was topped off with a bouquet of a dozen rose varying in colors from white, lavender, to the deepest purple all gathered together with a huge white ribbon with babies breathe showering the bouquet.

Tiffany looked at Jordan, he was more handsome than ever today, in his tailor made black tux, cool crisp white shirt, accented with a lavender bow tie and a single lavender rose with babies breath in his lapel and had his beard and mustache trimmed to just softly shadowing his face.

Once Jordan had finished singing, Rev. Nelson asked who was to give the bride away; Ken answered to announce himself then turned and winked at his baby girl as he moved aside. They proceeded with the exchanging of their vows and their magical kiss of forever they turned to the congregation and Rev. Nelson presented them to everyone as Mr. and Mrs. Jordan Alexander and they made their walk back down the isle as husband and wife.